Chapter One

Annette and her seven-year old son, Raynard, lived on the first floor flat of an old Georgian house in Westbourne Park Road in West London. The house belonged to a kindly old spinster from the Caribbean named Rosita Clements. The building stood on four floors which included a basement where Rosita Clements lived. The house had been beautifully redecorated recently. Each floor was a self-contained flat with hot and cold water; a small gas-cooker; carpeted and central heated.

Annette came from the Caribbean eighteen years ago. She met Raynard's father, also from the Caribbean, in London; they had a relationship and Raynard was the result. Raynard's father then took off to America.

Raynard's father lived in a world of make-believe. He was a womanizer and thought he was God's gift to women. He liked the idea of women looking after him, because he boasted that he was a great lover. He was crafty and conniving. The women never knew what he was up to, until he had taken them to bed and taken their money.

Annette was deeply in love with him. At first, she played hard to get, but he was good looking and made promises, had ambitions of making her the centre of his life. They kissed and cuddled for a long time; Annette wanted to see how long he could stand it. Whenever he tried to have sex with her she summoned all her strength and stopped him. Sometimes he would be angry or had a cold shower. He tried every trick he knew. He promised Annette the world but she never gave in. When finally they made love, it was so passionate that he cried like a baby when he had his orgasm. He did say that it was the sweetest sex he ever had, that the earth not only moved, it did somersaults; it was beyond ecstasy. Her body seemed to flame as she screamed her orgasm. He said that Annette was a glorious person, that with her he had discovered the deepest part of his being that his soul was being opened

A CARIBBEAN VAMPIRE IN LONDON

a novel by FAUSTIN CHARLES

Library of Congress Cataloguing-in-Publication Data

ISBN

978-1-910648-00-1

Published by GLOM Publications

Division of GLOM MEDIA, London

Designed and Printed by JSK Design & Print UK

"There are more things in heaven and earth, Horatio,
Than are dreamt of in your philosophy."

(HAMLET) Shakespeare.

AUTHOR'S NOTE

A "Soucouyant" is a blood-sucking vampire of Caribbean folk mythology. In the day-time it's an old woman who lives alone and is loved and respected by all in the community because she is always helpful. But at night, this unsuspecting loveable old woman peels off her skin like a garment, hides it, becomes a ball of fire and flies out into the night seeking her victims. The Soucouyant alights on the roof-top of her intended victim, enters unseen, bites the victim and sucks all the blood.

The Soucouyant must return and put on her skin and resume her human shape before morning; but if lots of raw rice grains are scattered in her path, and salt is put on her skin, the Soucouyant is doomed. She must count every grain of rice before the sun rises, and she cannot touch the skin because it will burn her. The Soucouyant talks to her skin, wails, and then shrivels up and dies. She is then put in a barrel of tar, burnt and the ashes thrown into the sea.

up. Yet when she got pregnant, he had disappeared. At first he lied and said that he got a job which was taking up all his time. The excuse was feeble and Annette had seriously thought of having an abortion. She got very ill, consumed with anger for all men. Friends were there to support and take care of her, especially Rosita Clements.

Annette decided to have the baby but she grew to distrust the world, even entertained a secret hatred. She went into a kind of sexual abstinence, something like the kind nuns exhibit. She steeled herself to bring up her baby. Her mother came from the Caribbean to live with them but died after three years in England. She used to baby sit and look after Raynard when he was a baby; she loved her grandson very much. Raynard was now nine years old.

Annette's mother's death seemed to shatter her sensibilities; she changed completely. She began to face the world with an entirely new face, a new kind of awareness and she was extremely cautious.

Rosita Clements was there for her, helping her look after her baby. She came into Annette's life at the right time. Rosita herself had had great disappointments with men, a series of miscarriages, family tragedy and society's disapproval. Finally, she had had enough and left all that behind and decided to try her luck in England. Maybe Rosita Clements saw in Annette the family she never had. Or maybe it was because both women shared the same of life's disappointments. Annette came out into the world as a mother figure. She didn't have many friends.

Sometimes Annette would rage in nightmares and also to Rosita: "Why he didn't love me! I'm not ugly!" And indeed she was very attractive. "I'm great in bed!" She knew how to use her body to the greatest effect when she made love. "The world isn't fair!"

As Raynard grew up, his father loomed in Annette's mind as an enemy to be crushed. She hated talking about him; all things such as presents, photographs, clothes that reminded her of him she burned and poured incense on the flames.

"You too wrapped up in hate, child!" Rosita Clements had warned. "That could be you undoing. You have to let go of all dat, man! De world not bad as you make out. And not all men like you child father. One day you'll meet a genuine one."

These words of Rosita soothed Annette outwardly but in the depths of her soul the fires of hate burned. She began to sense people, even to know their distant smells. Sometimes she thought she could taste what they had eaten.

"However you might hate and distrust people," Rosita had philosophised, "You must have friends in this world, especially in a cold, unfriendly place like England."

Annette had suitors but she never gave any of them the feeling that he was the only one in her life. Sometimes she played them against each other: sometimes they fought each other. She boasted to everyone about her independence.

Whenever Raynard asked about his father, Annette always had an excuse for him. She was tempted to say that his father was dead because she thought that it was better that he was dead.

Raynard wondered about his father but he loved his mother dearly and he saw that it pained her greatly when the subject of his father came up. He thought about the matter a lot. He was a sensitive child, bright at school. In his childhood fantasies he surmised that his father must have caused his mother a lot of pain for her to be hurt by the mere mention of his name. In fact, she was only angry with Raynard when the subject of his father came up. Otherwise she was a very loving mother to him. She used to say that she was both Raynard's father and mother. She spoilt him rotten and gave into his every childhood whim.

Since he didn't know his father, Raynard found it easy to make him only a tiny part of his memory.

Annette saw to it that Raynard was well looked after. Sometimes a smile, a grimace, a sigh, a frown in Raynard's face reminded her of his father. Whenever this happened she would go off to be alone for a moment so that she couldn't be overcome by the rage that bubbled and would have burst inside her.

With Rosita Clements' help, Annette had got a job and was coping the best she could with life. But she had an inward hunger for something more meaningful.

Rosita kept her distance from the tenants, and they

were never on long lets; leases were always short term. And she only saw them when they paid the rent and when there were repairs to be done. She said, "Good Morning!" "Good Afternoon!" or "Goodnight!" to all, that was all. She wasn't hard on any of her tenants: if they couldn't pay the rent, she understood and gave them time to pay. She never harassed them if they had parties, kept noise or invited friends or relatives to stay over sometimes for days even months on end.

She came to England with the Windrush generation. Her life in the Caribbean was a mystery. She never said from which island she came. Only that she had an extremely hard life, was treated badly by friends and family and migrated to England for a better life. She was always secretive about what she was doing. She did various jobs when she arrived in England: she was a cleaner on London transport and on British Rail; sometimes she worked at two jobs, working in the day and at night. She had very little time for boyfriends and seemed to have given up on the male sex. She had very few friends who were from the Caribbean; she never took part in the English way of life. She scraped and saved, denying herself luxuries and necessities to buy a house.

Rosita thought that Raynard should be told of his Caribbean origins; that this would sustain him and give him a sense of his own worth; that his state of being was fortified with knowledge of his cultural antecedents. Since England wasn't welcoming and all-embracing, it is important that Raynard's self-esteem be protected.

Annette, on the other hand, thought of herself as a modern British, woman and wanted her son to feel British. She appreciated Rosita Clements' interest in him, especially looking after him so that she had the freedom to go out whenever she chose.

"Miss Rosie fills the boy's head with a lot of Caribbean fairy-tale nonsense," she told a friend one day in the street. "I mean, the boy get carried away sometimes, thinking the stories are true, likes to be frightened to death."

"But don't you think it's good for the children born here to know about life in the Caribbean?" the friend said thoughtfully.

"What's that going to do for them!" Annette didn't mean to snap. "How is learning about the Caribbean going to help them to live and survive in England!"

The friend didn't know how to respond. After a while the friend shrugged and said, "Well, it can't do any harm, let's put it that way!"

"All it teaches is that we're different," Annette said hastily. "I know I'm different. In fact, everybody is different. I'm against it turning into a kind of apartheid, that's all. I don't want to live in the past; I feel I'm going backwards, that I'm backward. I want to move forward. I'm young and full of life. I don't want anything to keep me back. Not men, not anything about my mother and grandmother's past life"

The girlfriend brightened, "Well, you, and people like you want to live like English people. Like when in Rome do as the Romans do. But suppose we are doing as the Romans doing and the Romans still don't want us. What do we have to fall back on to give us strength and peace of mind? You and I both know the English don't want you here, they only treat us with cold tolerance. You need something to keep you sane. Some people go mad when they have to face rejection. You think this is the Mother Country, and you find out that you mother don't want you".

Annette thought for a long while before replying. "I mean the Caribbean past life. What has that got to do with me. If I have a past it's the past lives of people like me who came here as children or they were born here. There was black people living in this country centuries ago. I want to know how they lived. That's my past, that's my history."

"I don't mean we should live in the past," the friend seemed to relent.

"How the boy going to grow up!" Rosita Clements had said. "You must know where you come from before you know where you going! You carry what you is deep inside you all the time you on this earth. No matter what you do you can't change that!"

Annette's flat had a small bedroom which was Raynard's room; another bigger room which was hers; a small kitchen; a spacious sitting room-cum-dining room, and a bathroom and toilet. And a television in the sitting room area.

Annette worked in a working-men's café about quarter of a mile away.

Arthur Gawain lived on the third floor above Annette's. His parents were from the Caribbean. Unlike Annette, Gawain was proud of his Caribbean heritage. He was a popular masquerader in the Notting Hill Carnival, also one of the organisers on the committee. His costumes were always based on the legends and mythology of the Caribbean. He researched them thoroughly, even sometimes visiting various Caribbean islands. The talk every August Bank Holiday around Notting Hill was, "Who's going to beat Gawain!" Gawain was a gentle man, simple and quiet. He had been on television and radio several times talking about Carnival and its origins. His costumes were well-made, original and beautiful in a blaze of eye-catching colours that reminded people of the Caribbean flowers, butterflies and birds. Although he was born in England, Gawain affected a Caribbean accent some of the time. Most of the time, he ate Caribbean foods and in summer, wore clothes of dazzlingly bright Caribbean colours.

Gawain was friendly to all in the house. He took a fancy to Joycelyn, but kept quiet about it, because he too often overheard what she and Annette thought about men particularly Caribbean men. He thought it best to wait for the right time to make his move.

He was always there for everyone in the house: to offer help, advice or even financial assistance. He also told Caribbean folk stories to Raynard.

"Ray, I use to love the stories told me about Caribbean ghosts and demons!" his face widened into the brightest enthusiasm. "I was always frightened, but the way my mother told them was like magic and she made me understand that they weren't real, they were only make-believe fairytales. So in the end I always enjoyed them."

"That's how Miss Rosie tells them!" Raynard's eyes would almost pop out his head. "It's almost like if the stories were true. She makes them come to life. Then she'll laugh and say they're not true."

"Boy, only people from the Caribbean can tell stories like that," Gawain would break into a most joyous Caribbean laugh.

Raynard knew a lot about Caribbean folk stories much to his mother's dismay.

Gawain also pleaded with Annette to let Raynard take part in the Carnival.

"It'll be dangerous. I'm not taking that risk," Annette responded. " The Children's Carnival does get a little too wild sometimes."

"And I keep telling you he'll be alright!" Gawain always reassured her. "The police and the stewards look after the children very well. Of course, I'll always be there for him. Many children take part in the Carnival. They love dancing and having fun. It'll be great. I'll take good care of him."

Raynard was overjoyed.

"Oh, mum, that'll be cool!" he beamed like the sun rising from his face.

"I don't know," Annette turned away. I'll think about it."

Every available space in Gawain's flat was littered with photographs of costumes, drawings of costumes, bits and pieces of velvet, satin, lace, fur, peacock feathers, sequins and rhinestones. And balls of string, bottles of glue, wire, ribbons and small tins of paint of every colour.

Annette's best friend was a slim, attractive woman of thirty who was married in England in her early twenties her husband had left her and returned to the Caribbean. She visited Annette frequently, and was the only one of Annette's friends to do so. Jocelyn was childless. Sometimes she would baby-sit Raynard. She lived in Kilburn.

One day around noon, Annette and Jocelyn were talking. It was mid May bright with the Spring sunshine sparkling on happy faces.

"You mean, she don't mind at all!" Jocelyn didn't mean to raise her voice, realised it and soften her tone. "When I rented a flat not far from here some years ago; the landlord had a list of don'ts" like the "Ten Commandments." He was very strict. He only wanted one man-friend at a time to visit me. Girl, he behaved like a fussy father."

"But that's like him choosing your boyfriend for you!" Annette's eyes widen with amazement. "Maybe he fancied you, ha! Ha! Ha!"

"Hah! I don't think so," Jocelyn smiled. "He wasn't that sort of bloke. He had a wife and four children and faithful to the end. And he believed in one man, one wife, or one man, one woman."

"Well, Miss Clements isn't like that at all," Annette beamed. "I'm not saying she doesn't care if you burn down the house. But she's very kind and considerate. She realises that young people must have freedom and fun. After all, she was young once."

"What! She tell you that!" Jocelyn exclaimed, overwhelmed.

"I heard she telling tenants. I'm lucky to have a landlady like her. I think it's because we're from the Caribbean. From the first time we met, Miss Clements and I liked each other."

Did you see Ricky last night?" Jocelyn chuckled, changing the subject.

Annette's face changed from that of being calm and relaxed into seriousness and even anger.

"The other night he came here. I wasn't in the mood for no damn stupidness," Annette's face hardened as she spoke. He pulled at my clothes, tear me dress. That blasted good- for-nothing!"

The two women laughed for about forty minutes. The laughter came from the depths of their souls.

Chapter two

One windy, biting evening in late February, Raynard said to his mother, "Mum, Miss Clements knows so many stories. She knows more stories than Mr Gawain. She even knows more than granny used to."

"Aren't you tired of such stories," Annette replied, and looking out of a window and changing the subject, said, "I wonder if we're going to have a storm."

"You mean like a hurricane in the Caribbean!" Raynard stared wide-eyed out of the window.

It was as if the house was shaking. Annette's face clouded, her whole body shook to the whirling rhythm of the winds.

"Granny used to say a hurricane can sweep everything away!" Raynard trembled as he spoke. "Grown-ups get frightened and run and hide. Children cry and get very sick. She said that it was like the world coming to an end. Nobody knows what to do in a hurricane."

"God forbid, boy," Annette bent and checked a radiator.

I don't think your granny had ever been in a hurricane. May her soul rest in peace."

Rain pelted, then poured, and it became a trifle warm, but the winds persisted.

It had snowed for most of February: one of the worse winters on record. Caribbean people cursed the winter.

By the end of February, the snow thawed; the weather was a mixture of high winds, rain and sleet.

One summer's night, Raynard swore he saw an apparition flying through the sky like a bird, a black fiery bird. He had rubbed his eyes again and again until the apparition was gone. He thought he had allowed his imagination to run away with him.

"Boy de stories and them have you dreaming all kinda strange things dat you think is real!" Gawain laughed as he spoke in a humorous Caribbean accent.

Rosita Clements stopped telling Raynard scary stories; the stories were still from the Caribbean, but they were all cheerful with happy endings.

Annette was happy.

Raynard's imagination still ran riot!

One night, Raynard was lost in a story, carried away by Rosita's telling when she rose from an armchair and said, "Awright, boy, time you go up to you mother to sleep now!"

Raynard didn't hear at first, he was in a state of magical dizziness. He sat, unable to rise, trembling, trying to speak but his voice didn't obey him.

"What happen, boy, you think de story true!" Rosita laughed, intending to quell any fear that might have arisen in him.

Raynard finally got to his feet, wobbled and stuttered, "Time for bed, Miss Rosie. I'm feeling tired and sleepy. You're a great storyteller. Thank you very much. Goodnight Miss Rosie. I like all the stories, yes Goodnight."

Rosita Clements was smiling and shaking her head. Raynard yawned, turned and staggered out of the room. "You're always welcome, boy, but you mustn't take de story so serious, they only fairytales," Rosita smiled widely.

Raynard's sleep was filled with dreams of animals turning into people and vice versa. One night he dreamt something like an animal was breathing against his face, smelling his every breath. It was a very hot night. He woke up perspiring and was astonished to discover a firefly flying about his room, trying desperately to get out, knocking on the window wildly.

Raynard quickly opened the window, and it flew out. At breakfast he said to his mother, "I didn't know there were fireflies in England?"

Annette sighed and replied, "You've been dreaming again. Of course, there aren't any such things in this country." She then laughed and said, "Only if one flew out of a Caribbean fairytale"

"Yes, it was only a dream," he mumbled, his head bowed.

Chapter Three

Then it began! All over Ladbroke Grove, people, mostly children were bitten, their blood drained at once or over a long period. All the victims underwent a strange transformation. Their face showed utter shock and terror; straight hair became curly; curly hair became straight. Their skins changed; limbs became soft and fragile. Everything in the body seemed to be liquidized. Eyes popped out of sockets; throats and stomachs were torn open. And in the cases of the male victims, penises and testicles were bitten off and stuffed in the mouths and anuses.

The authorities thought it was a strange blood disease carried by an insect or animal because sometimes there were animal teeth-marks or insect bites on victims, necks, arms, chests or stomach. They also noted that the strange disease reached its height in the summertime.

Some people put crucifix around their doors and windows. They believed in a kind of blood-sucking vampire bat.

Most people in the Ladbroke Grove area were afraid to go out at night, and kept their homes tightly shut and sealed.

"They makin' fuss outa nothing," Rosita Clements said to Annette one day when Annette came to pay the rent.

"But....but....it....it sounds like a wild animal attacking people and sucking their blood," Annette shuddered. "There're so many disgusting things happening in the world these days. Sometimes I'm afraid for me and my son."

"Dat's nonsense, me dear," Rosita smiled. "People does believe in nonsense. In this day and age, you can't get thing like dat. If you ask me, it's all them horror film on television. Everybody seein' monsters flying about and attacking them nowadays."

You're right, Miss Clement," Annette relaxed. "Somebody is pretending to be a blood-sucking monster they saw on television. And then, it could be all to do with drugs: when people take these drugs they feel they can do anything. But I'm sure it's nothing contagious." Annette's face became thoughtful.

The newspapers had a great time with headlines such as; "VAMPIRE STRIKES IN LONDON," "ANOTHER UNEXPLAINED FOREIGN DISEASE," "BLOOD BUG KILLER," "DRUG–CRAZED BLOOD-SUCKERS IN LONDON," and "DRACULA IS ALIVE AND WELL AND LIVING IN LADBROKE GROVE."

And the fact was, a monster, a blood-sucking monster of Caribbean origin called "Soucouyant," living a make-believe life as a human-being, wrapped in its ancient skin of horror and deceit, felt that it could never be discovered in this country. Every summer it swirled through the night with its voracious appetite for blood.

An old woman who had had some terrible injustice done to her, was unleashing a blood-feast, blood thirsty revenge on all around her. She also enjoyed the long life and power the evil Soucouyant-transformation gave her. The transformation from middle or old age to monster took place at night. Her hair became wild and unkempt; eyes blood-red and piercing; mouth protruding; teeth long, pointed and razor-sharp, and tongue very long and slimy. Then the skin peeled off from head to toes, and fingers and toes became claw-like. Then it hid the skin, turned into a firefly and as it ascended the sky it became a ball of fire.

The Soucouyant laughed loudly in its fiery bosom, and muttered, "They never going to find me out. Heh! heh! heh! heh! because they too stupid. They feel they all clever with their big science, but I fool them every time." Every summer when the sun blazed down on London, it left a mystery of blood-drained bodies in its wake.

Doctors were completely baffled. None of them believed nor entertained the idea that it was a vampire blood sucker or any such thing. Their prognosis was that it was a blood disorder, triggered by a wound like a cut or bruise.

One Saturday noon in early June, Ricky, Annette's friend, knocked on the front door, and was let in by Raynard.

"Mummy isn't in," Raynard said sulkily; he knew about the situation between his mother and Ricky.

Ricky was a tall, handsome, well-built man in his early thirties.

"That door-bell out there don't work," Ricky frowned.

Sometimes the front door isn't locked," Raynard said timidly. "It's doors to the flats that are locked all the time."

"That's very trusting. You're here on your own?"

"The landlady is looking after me. She's in the basement."

"You don't mind if I wait for your mother, it's important that I see her," Ricky's voice was strained and serious.

"No, I don't mind."

Raynard and Ricky went into the sitting-room area.

Ricky sprawled himself in an armchair.

Raynard went to his room.

The early June sun twinkled through the windows; it was a cold June beginning.

Ricky thought of smoking but decided not to. He was uncomfortable. He rose, stood for a few minutes, then sat down again.

When Annette came home, her son came out to greet her happily. Ricky rose and smiled widely at her.

Annette and Raynard put away the shopping. Then with an ice cream and a packet of crisps, Raynard went back to his room.

Annette came into the sitting-room area, sighed heavily and said, "What do you want?"

"Ann, darling, I'm sorry if I done wrong," Ricky tried to keep his voice within the confines of the room with little success. "You know that you're the only one I love!"

"And you prove that by sleeping with everything in a skirt!" Annette raised her voice probably to match his.

"I don't do that. It's dangerous nowadays with Aids about!" Ricky stood up.

"So it's because it's dangerous, uh. You're afraid you get Aids not because you're faithful to me!" Annette couldn't control her anger.

"No, no, I didn't mean it like that at all!" Ricky sat back down.

"Jocelyn told me that she saw you kissing that Italian woman in the alley by the Royal Hunt Pub. You can't deny it. She saw you!"

"It was just a friendly, platonic kiss, that was all," Ricky tried to smile but failed.

"What do you want from me, because I've things to do," Annette waved her hand.

"Don't be like that! I want to invite you out tonight," Ricky's tone was now humble, meek and mild.

Annette thought for a long while, calmed herself, relaxed in a seat facing him.

"Jocelyn said that she would baby-sit Raynard," this time Ricky was successful with a smile. "I mean, you can't always ask your landlady."

For a while neither of them spoke, they only stared at each other. Mixed feelings filled Annette's mind. Whatever his faults, deep in her soul she felt the rage welling up inside her again, but she controlled and calmed herself.

Raynard came in and broke the silence.

Ricky rose, certain of himself and said, "I'll see you tonight," and made towards the flat-door.

Annette agreed to go out with Ricky. That evening, Jocelyn came and baby-sat Raynard.

Annette enjoyed herself. She and Ricky went dancing, then to supper at a Chinese Restaurant in the West End. It was almost two o'clock in the morning when they returned to Ladbroke Grove.

"Your son has a weird imagination," Jocelyn told Annette. "He told me stories about men and women turning into beasts."

Annette laughed and phoned a minicab to take Jocelyn home.

Ricky nodded off on the settee.

Jocelyn whispered something to Annette about him; Annette shrugged.

Raynard was sound asleep when his mother checked on him.

The minicab came quickly. Annette saw Jocelyn to the door. Without waking Rick, Annette went to bed.

Ricky woke up at eight o'clock in the morning, making a great fuss about an insect bite on his arm.

"I can't remember bumping into anything or bruising it against anywhere, "he moaned as he showed the marks to Annette.

There were teeth-marks and a wound like a bite, the blood had clotted.

"It's like a dog-bite," Raynard said playfully.

"I wonder if it's one of them vampire bats that got loose from London Zoo and it's feeding around here! Oh, God, I hope not, they must spread disease," Ricky shrieked.

Ricky lived in Willesden Green.

Annette bathed the wound with dettol, then put TCP and bandaged it.

"When you have children you have to be ready for all emergencies," she muttered as she tended Ricky, nurse-like.

You probably bruise your hand and you can't remember, that's what it was; it happens all the time to people."

"I'm going to the doctor later on," Ricky went on moaning. "It could be that blood-draining sickness people are talking about that is happening around this area."

"Don't get carried away, man," Annette snapped. "You wouldn't lose your life or your hand because of a little cut. I tell you, somebody or something scratched you and you were probably a little drunk, so you didn't notice it."

But Ricky spent a long time in a frantic state, even though the doctor told him it was only an insect bite. He didn't like going to Ladbroke Grove anymore. Whenever he and Annette met, they met in the West End or at his home.

July was very hot, the sky was the clearest blue, and the heat went on far into the night.

The Soucouyant was happy in the wonder of its succulent soul. Its skin thrilled, its body rippled with the instinct of new blood. The human-part of it muttered in ecstacy, "Oh, the sun ripe up me hungry. I must fly in the hot night and full meself with lots of new blood."

"Girl, I am thinking seriously of moving out of

Ladbroke Grove," Jocelyn was trembling, her eyes darkening, her face weary.

"Why, don't be so stupid, girl!" Annette frowned. "All that blood-sucking vampire business, it's only the newspaper printing nonsense."

"Some people did move out, you hear," Jocelyn seemed distant. "Everybody afraid to go out at night, even the police scared to be out."

"Well, I think people are just behaving like frightened little children," Annette shrugged. "And Ricky is too much of a coward for a grown man. He told me he's never coming back to Ladbroke Grove."

"So the two of you are back again, then?" Jocelyn changed the subject.

"Well, let's say, I'm giving him his last chance. If he slips up again, I'll tell him to get lost!"

Jocelyn felt an awful sense of tension.

In mid-June of the following summer, two policemen were patrolling a dark cul-de-sac: the area was quiet and completely deserted. They saw a ball of fire swirling about six feet above them; then the object came and hovered over their heads about a foot high. At first, they thought that it was a helicopter or a barn-owl, or maybe a meteorite, but then the object moved away and hovered for a long time over a block of flats, then it disappeared. The policemen couldn't believe their own eyes; they thought they had seen a UFO. They were completely mystified.

In the morning, a child was found dead, drained of all its blood in one of the flats in the block. The terror on the mutilated child's face frightened the skin off the onlookers. Its throat was torn or bitten out. The stomach was bitten out. The hair on the head stood straight from being once curly, and the colour of the skin changed from dark-brown to pink.

Chapter Four

In another part of Ladbroke Grove, the Soucouyant became human, got up early the following morning with the sun in its soul. Whoever it was, felt safe and strong with the ripening blood of many victims. In its deepest self the sun shone mightily. It was indeed invincible in England.

All people from the Caribbean moved with an unbelievable ecstasy in summer. It was as if they were born again, rejuvenated with a life the host community could never understand.

The sun, hot, streamed through windows and lit up rooms everywhere. Outside, the air sparkled with green, and the sky was magical in its bluest. Birds twittered here and there.

The Soucouyant in its liar, wherever that was, licked its cruel lips. Deep in its innermost being, the sun burned and aggravated its thirst. It played with idea of conquering the whole of the Ladbroke Grove area and then moving on.

Midnight on a Saturday, the ball of fire of the Soucouyant streaked off into the cool night; the sky bright with stars and patches of white cloud. Higher and higher it soared into a night it thought was going to be a feast of blood.

It swooped down on a semi-detached house in the Holland Park area. Perched on the roof, it surveyed the scene. Then it entered through a window which was left half opened to let in air because of the hot weather. It came into a large spacious sitting-room, made it to the bed room; it seemed to be guided to the bedroom by instinct.

A man and his wife laid on the bed. The Soucouyant bit the man who was a little restless and sucked. The man wriggled a bit then became still. The wife stirred. The Soucouyant was absolutely quiet on the man's throat. The man passed out. Then his wife was bitten on the side of her face, under the right ear; she emitted groans as she was being sucked, then she too passed out.

The Soucouyant then went to the other bedrooms of two teenage sons. They were bitten and sucked, both moaned as if in a bad dream, then became unconscious.

In the morning, father, mother and sons were in a terrible state. The four of them quarrelled, raged at each other, blamed each other and almost fought and almost went mad with fear. They sweated and trembled profusely;,vomited and had urinal problems and diarrhoea.

The following day, three babies, a young man, and a young woman were bitten and their blood sucked. The babies were critically ill in hospital. All the victims changed colour, their faces contorted in sheer terror. The babies' throats and stomachs had large bites where chunks of flesh were removed.

About midnight, a bright flash lit-up outside the window of a house near to where Jocelyn lived. The landlord looked out and saw a ball of fire rolling towards the window. He was excited, the adrenalin flowing. The ball of fire came to the window, changed into a firefly and struck the pane hard and cracked it, then the firefly soared heavenward.

Hours later, the Soucouyant in its lair, snarled; "They can't kill me! They ain't know how to kill me! I go live forever in this place!" It growled and spat blood. Then it resumed its human shape, its human disguise.

People began suspecting each other; neighbour kept watch on neighbour. Someone in the area and its surroundings was wearing a mask, a costume of deception. Was it a young or old person? Male or female?

Some people carried weapons: knives, swords, even guns; others carried crucifixes, holy water and Bibles.

The police combed the area but never found who or what was responsible.

Some people still believed that it was all a scare, perpetrated by pranksters. Others, that were drug-crazed addicts and thieves who were rampaging through Ladbroke Grove.

Jocelyn still visited Annette, and Raynard and his friends were fascinated by it all. But Ricky wouldn't venture into the area anymore.

"Some people are soulless cowards, they'll believe any rubbish especially what they see on telly," Annette said to Jocelyn one morning in the autumn of the same year. Raynard was at school. Annette was getting ready for work when Jocelyn dropped in.

"Somebody's playing the fool, and the joke is getting outa hand, yes," Jocelyn was mournful. "When some people out of work, the devil will always find something for them to do."

"You know, sometimes Raynard wants to sleep in my bedroom, he gets afraid. I've told him that it's all nonsense," Annette laughed.

"Well he's a child, but Ricky is a real coward," the other woman grinned. " "With all his big macho-talk, he's frightened like a little child."

"Yes, dear, he said he loves me, that I'm the only one for him, that he can't live without me, yet he's shit scared to come around here to see me. Why do men treat me that way."

"That's men all the time, girl; big talk and showing off to get what they want. When they get it, they leave you."

Annette's face was wretched.

In the summertime, Ricky ventured back into the area, but only in the day-time; by six o'clock in the evening he was gone. He was absolutely convinced that a wild animal was on the prowl in Ladbroke Grove. There were others who shared his belief.

"Maybe it escape from the zoo," he was telling Annette and Raynard one Sunday lunch-time. "Or, it could be a pet tiger or other big cat that got away and attacking people. It tasted human blood somehow and now it's going mad for more and more. Some people have some strange animals for pets in this country!"

"Yes, mum , that could be it," Raynard spoke as he spooned roast potatoes onto his plate.

"I still say it's somebody doing some kind of prank," Annette said wearily. "Ricky, I'd like you to look after Ray for me today. I don't know the exact time I'm going to get away today?"

"Wha! You working today, man!" Ricky sputtered. "I mean, it's Sunday. They working you hard on Sunday too." He spilt some orange-juice he was drinking in surprise. "You don't even get Sunday off, man. It's suppose to be the day of rest. Alright, alright, I'll stay with the boy until you get back, but don't leave it late. I want to be outa this area before it gets dark."

"A grown man like you behaving like a child," Annette teased, "believing in a lot of silly talk."

"I don't care what you say. If you come back late, I'll have to sleep here. I don't want to be in this area in the night," Ricky stuttered.

"Alright, little boy afraid of the dark, afraid of the big bad bird. Mummy will be back early," Annette carried on teasing. "Mummy wouldn't let the fire-bird eat you!" Raynard laughed, spilling his food.

"Ray, don't play the fool with food!" Annette scolded her son rather too harshly. "Clean up your mess, you hear!" Raynard, startled, did as he was told quickly.

"The landlady doesn't mind if you sleep over here," Annette went on to Ricky. Don't worry, I'll be back from work early before it gets dark."

In the Soucouyant's secret place, it's stomach rumbled with the sun, the sum total of expectation. It was getting late:half-past five, then quarter to six, then six o'clock. Ricky was ill at ease. Raynard noticed his discomfiture.

"It's going to be alright," he reassured his anxious baby-sitter.

There was a loud shriek outside from the street.

Ricky jumped and said, "What was that, man!" his mouth twisting.

"Maybe a dog or cat," Raynard the child calmed the adult.

But as it grew later and later, Ricky knew he had to sleep at Annette's.

"Mum is working over-time," mused Raynard. "I think it happened before. She didn't know until late that she had to work for someone."

"That's why she should've had a telephone. You're always left with baby-sitters, you never know what can happen."

"A telephone or mobile-phone would be nice, yes," Raynard beamed.

Ricky shrugged, "Well, I have to sleep here, thats all.

Raynard nodded.

"I think your mother likes to play games with me sometimes. I bet she's having a right old laugh at me." Ricky looked out the window.

"It's going to be alright," Raynard smiled.

Annette arrived home at eight-thirty. She was busy and apologetic." I'm sorry, Rick, two people didn't turn up for work, so I had my hands full. Didn't Ray tell you it happened before. I didn't know until I was ready to come home. They left it until the last minute to say they couldn't come to work. Some people don't have consideration for others. It's times like these I wish I had a phone."

"Yes, Ray told me," Ricky frowned. "You should've said something about the possibility of this happening and don't expect Raynard to tell me. I'll have to sleep here, although I'm frightened like hell. I'm not going outside to phone a minicab. If this is a joke you're playing, I'm not laughing."

Ricky was more scared than angry.

Ricky slept on the couch. He was snoring profusely in the dead of midnight, when suddenly the snoring stopped.

45

A large firefly appeared, covered his face and bit him and sucked his blood. But it was a silent feeding. Ricky was completely unconscious. Neither Annette nor Raynard heard anything.

In the morning there was a large scream! Annette found Ricky unconscious with a large bite on his throat. He was rushed to the hospital and given a blood transfusion. For two and a half weeks he laid in a coma.

Annette wept and blamed herself.

Raynard was terrified and sad, but his friends thought that it was a bad bee-sting.

Rosita Clements consoled and comforted Annette and Raynard.

Rosita remarked that it was all silly people making up silly stories about blood-sucking summer insects.

The police came, searched the entire building and surroundings; they questioned Rosita, Annette and Raynard and Gawain.

Then Ricky died.

Annette was in a state of shock, and wanted to move out of the area. She was in hospital receiving treatment.

One night she had a dream of her dead mother who told her: "Men is no good. They does deceive you. Ricky was no good. He was only fooling you. He had a lotta women all over de place. De world can be a damn unreasonable place, watch you step, me daughter. Like they all hate you.Get well soon, me dearie. I hope Raynard well!"

When Raynard and Jocelyn saw Annette the following day, she relayed the dream shamelessly:

"I had a dream last night. It was about my mother; she was telling me that she hoped Raynard and me are okay. She said that Ricky was a no good womanizer."

"That maybe so, girl," Jocelyn was morose, "but it was a horrible way to die."

Annette hugged and kissed her son.

"Do you want me to bring you anything, mum?" asked Raynard anxiously.

"Yes, we were saying, is there any clothes or food you want us to bring!" Jocelyn seemed drained.

"Yes, bring the blue and green dressing gown," Annette too seemed utterly drained. "And some underwear, they're in the bottom drawer of the cupboard in my bedroom.

Raynard sighed heavily and looked away.

"The doctor thinks I might be anaemic," Annette's voice trembled. "He said I must eat a balanced diet. I might have to have some tests."

"Your body run down with a lot of stress, that's all," Jocelyn was almost angry. "And girl, I know you're not worried about what's happening in Ladbroke grove, but better watch yourself."

Raynard shuddered.

Annette sucked her teeth loudly and said, "I have to eat properly, and I think I'll start taking a tonic." .

When Annette got better, Rosita was extremely understanding, she had a telephone installed in the hallway.

Whenever she came to visit in the hospital, she had always said, "You mustn't worry. You must take life easy. We people must stick together in this country. Don't worry about money and bills, I go give you plenty time to pay me." She did look after Raynard sometimes.

"I told you that she is an agreeable landlady,"

Annette said to Jocelyn smilingly.

Sometimes Annette left Raynard in Jocelyn's care, she was almost like a second mother to him.

One night in the middle of June, Jocelyn was babysitting Raynard. She was watching television. Raynard was fast asleep in his room. She heard a knocking on the window, went to investigate and saw a flash of bright light, then a firefly was bumping against the pane.

"Oh God, it's that thing!" She was confused, so she began to perspire and tremble. Her heart drummed in her chest. All kinds of thoughts raced through her mind, as she shook out of her skin with fear. Her heart drummed louder than ever! Her chest heaved, and she was wet all over.

"Oh, God, save me, Sweet Son, Jesus, Saviour, have mercy on me! Don't let it bite me!" she chattered. Her eyes were popping out of her head as she stared at the object; then she swayed and fainted in a heap on the floor.

After this incident, she became very afraid and seldom visited Annette.

One day at noon at the end of May, she met Annette

for lunch. They sat in a Mcdonald's café not far from where Annette worked. They wanted to talk without interruptions. It was Annette's lunch-break.

"Ann, I don't think I want to come to your place anymore," she began, lips twitching. "This blood sucker tried to attack me at your place. It's after me, it's going to try again, oh God."

"What bloody rubbish! I've told you before it's that film you were watching on television that night." Annette lost her cool for a while. "It's still freaking you out, I tell you. It was only a bad dream you've had. You must have dozed off while watching the television, and you were between sleep and wake as they say. You were so taken in by the film and got carried away."

"What about how Ricky died, then?!" Jocelyn felt cold, a chill ran down her spine, she shivered visibly.

"Get a hold of yourself, girl. Ricky used to drink and womanise too much. Who knows what disease he picked up, maybe it was a kind of Aids. Maybe he was into drugs. It was sad how he died, but as they say, how you live, so you die."

"But.....but....you....you...was so upset, you was falling to pieces. You ended up in hospital," Jocelyn didn't mean to get angry.

"Of course, I was upset. He was a very close friend who got sick in my flat. I was and still am very sorry. But I've come to realise that it was his fault. Maybe he was poisoned by one of his gangster friends."

"You wasn't there, girl, you don't know what I went through. All I know now is I have to be very careful."

"I don't know what has become of the people of Ladbroke Grove, like they've all gone mad; nasty things are happening, I admit, but weird and nasty things are happening all over the world. I don't know what has come over you. It was a nightmare you had!"

Jocelyn visited Annette in the daytime only.

One Saturday, Raynard came from Gawain's flat bubbling over with excitement. Gawain not only told him folk stories from the Caribbean, but all about carnival.

"Mum, Mr Gawain is a very nice man!" Raynard couldn't contain himself as he told his mother. "He was telling me about how they celebrate carnival in the Caribbean. You know, mum, they have children's carnival. And they have a competition where the children get prizes for the best costumes. That's great, isn't it!"

"That's very nice dear," Annette was disinterested. Raynard bowed his head and felt a deep yearning, as if the songs, colours and happiness were reaching out to touch him.

One midday, Annette ,Jocelyn and Gawain met in the hallway outside Annette's flat just as Annette and Jocelyn were about to enter.

"Hello, how's everything!" Gawain blushed as he looked at Jocelyn. And to Annette, "You have a very bright son. He's kind and respectful. You're a great mother."

"I do my best," Annette smiled.

"I know how hard it must be to raise a child on your own in an area like this."

Jocelyn nodded smilingly.

Gawain leaned on the banister as he spoke to Jocelyn, "Joyce I heard you're afraid to come here in the night. That's nonsense. You mustn't let any crazy people upset your life, man."

Annette looked at both of them and said, "How about a cup of tea?" And she opened her door.

"Yes, yes, if one's going, yes," Gawain stuttered.

"That'll be nice," Jocelyn said, still smiling.

And they both followed Annette into her flat.

Chapter five

Darwin Stevenson came into Annette's life about this time. He wasn't like Ricky nor any of her other boyfriends. He was tall, about six feet, five inches, and very handsome; and always dressed in a suit. He carried his mobile-phone even when he went to the bathroom. Also he was very hard-working and ambitious.

Annette was nervous when she first met him: he had dropped into her place of work to get a cup of coffee. Annette had goose-pimples all over, and stuttered all the time. She kept smiling at him, and he took that bait and kept coming to the café at least once a week. When he finally popped a question to her, she melted.

"I'd like to take you out to dinner, Miss?" he was straight to the point but respectful.

"Annette is my name. Why.....yeeeessssssyes...

thank....you, yes....I'd...I'd like to....".

"And my name is, Darwin," and he smiled with his whole attractive personality, Annette thought.

They wined and dined at a fashionable restaurant in the West End.

Annette had never wined and dined before. She was nervous and fidgety all through the meal which was three courses.

Darwin Stevenson was an accountant in a reputable firm in the city. He was a very determined young man. He lived in his own flat in West Hampstead.

"I do my shopping in Ladbroke Grove," he began, "I like the shops, especially the Caribbean shops. Do you like Caribbean food?"

"Yes, sometimes I cook it, yes," Annette blushed. "I like it sometimes as well," Darwin laughed. His parents came from Barbados and Jamaica. He was born in London. He was three years older than Annette.

"My son doesn't like it at all, and when I get the chance I cook it for myself, and things like fish-fingers and chips, I cook for him."

"What does your husband think of it?" Darwin wanted everything out in the open. I don't mean to pry into your business, please, maybe I shouldn't........I'm...."

"No, no, it's alright," Annette cut in. "I wasn't married when I had my son, and his father and I aren't together. I live with my only son, in a flat not far from here; and yes, my son's father loved Caribbean food, in fact, he loved all foods as long as he didn't have to cook it."

Darwin smiled then laughed merrily.

They dined on lobsters, crab, chicken, potatoes, salad, plum pudding and white wine.

They had a wonderful time; Annette thought she deserved it after her recent grief.

When Darwin brought her home in his BMW car, Rosita peered through the window into the night at them; she had baby-sat Raynard who was now asleep.

The following morning was Sunday towards the end of Spring: there had been some hot days peeping through at that time of year.

Annette woke up with a song in her heart as well as

in her voice.

"What sweeten you so, girl?" her landlady said, after knocking loudly, and was told to come in.

"I'm in love, Miss Clements!" crooned Annette as she began to prepare breakfast.

"Oh, that what it is, eh," Rosita Clements smiled. "Who's the lucky man, then?" she asked, pretending not to know.

"You must have seen him around, his name is Darwin Stevenson!" Annette's face seemed to light up with a mysterious magic. "He's so good, understanding, trusting, and he's well-off."

"So, you think he go marry you?" Rosita was still smiling. "After all, you have child. Do you think he go want look after another man child."

"Well, maybe, I don't know. I mean, he's understanding and very kind."

"And what about your freedom and independence you always talking about. You used to say you don't want no man to tie you down and rule you life."

"Maybe it's now time for a change. Maybe the right

man has come, and it's time to settle down. I don't want to be working in that caf all my life. I have to seriously think of me and my son's future."

Rosita Clements tried to understand.

"Men does show very nice face and nice manners. And when you give up everything and settle down with them, they does change into the most horrible human beings," she finally said.

"I'm not saying that Darwin is a saint, but when I'm with him I feel safe and secure."

"I was never lucky with men. And I like me independence."

"Oh, I'm thinking about it long and before I commit myself," Annette's voice wavered, her face became very serious. She understood her landlady's advice. But she would never tolerate any critisism of her beloved Darwin.

Rosita nodded and smiled again.

Darwin was indeed gifted. He had a baritone voice and he knew how to modulate it in anger and joy. The way he saw the world, the way he explained things to Annette made her feel special. Raynard's father and Ricky had never touched her that way. Darwin was very clever at working out problems which at first seemed insurmountable. Most of the time he was the diplomat rather than the fighter, but he wasn't a coward. He thought long and hard before he spoke, formulating every detail in his mind.

"I never knew there was such men about," Annette said. "It's almost as if he isn't real."

Whenever they made love, it was as if Darwin was being sucked into her. It was absolutely incredible. At first he felt like he was floating on air, in fact, they were both off the bed, sofa and off the floor, sailing high in the sky. When their orgasms came, they were like a million suns shining through their bodies and blasting them to another dimension. It was sweetness beyond ordinary human experience.

Darwin knew how to enjoy himself; a good joke always brought belly laughs that rocked his whole body.

"I'm never going to promise you what I can never give you," Darwin once said to Annette, kissing her neck and ears as he spoke. "What I have and what I am are what I'll offer you always. I'm not perfect. And you're going to find out all my faults. I'll never hide them from you. I have an open mind about life."

Darwin's parents taught him nothing of Caribbean life and culture; only the food which they cooked most of the time which he always enjoyed. He heard them speaking their Caribbean language but some of the time he found it difficult to understand.

One night he was returning home from Ladbroke Grove when he saw a light dancing outside a window at the top of a four-storeyed building. At first he thought it was a flashlight but then it fluttered like a bird. He had heard about the strange occurrences in Ladbroke Grove.

He stopped the car, came out, stood by the car and made out a pigeon-sized firefly knocking against the window-pane.

"Is that insect or bird?" he thought. "It's glowing like a firefly." He began to think deeply about the strange occurrences. "So it's true about these firefly creatures. Such a big one! This is extremely strange! The environment is so mucked up; maybe that's what is causing all these weird creatures to appear."

Then the light went out, the firefly disappeared.

Darwin stood there thinking for a while, his eyes searching the surroundings then he drove off.

The following morning, a baby's head bitten from its body was discovered; it was sucked dry of blood to the skull. The parents were in a terrible state and were in the hospital.

Only a few people, and they were of the older generation, took the idea of a blood-sucking vampire roaming the area seriously. Most people, especially the young, laughed at such superstition. The scientists and doctors speculated that it might be some sort of blood disease spread by a mysterious tropical insect or bird that flies to Britain in the summer.

Unknown to even Annette, Darwin began to take a deep interest in the macabre occurrences that were going on around the area. He was tactful and shrewd. Since everybody, except his beloved Annette, were under suspicion, he thought it best to be secretive in his investigations. Sometimes he shuddered when he comprehended the incidents but he always managed to keep his composure. Two things he was certain of, one, the evil blood-sucker was female because of the way it mutilated the sexual organs of its male victims, and two, that it operated on summer nights. He was going to be a master "detective" in solving these dastardly crimes.

Meanwhile, the Soucouyant, was very careful. It now ventured out of the Ladbroke Grove area and fed to satiety on the blood of adults only. It waited for the fuss and publicity to die away.

People still saw "fire-balls" in the sky, of which the authorities explained as "shooting stars" or meteorites.

Whoever the Soucouyant was, felt a great contentment, because it reasoned that no one in England and Europe knew anything about it and how to destroy it. When it soared it seemed to reach high heaven in its ecstacy and deepest joy.

One July morning at breakfast, Annette was buttering toast. Rosita Clements was there.

"There's some weird things going on in this Ladbroke Grove," Annette said in a strange way.

Raynard looked at his mother thoughtfully and ate his food slowly.

"Every part of dis London there's always something strange or out de ordinary going on. With all these new drugs going around, it weird like hell," Rosita said with the heaviest of sighs.

"Darwin thinks it's very strange as well. I hope he doesn't stop coming," Annette's voice suddenly full of sorrow as she remembered Ricky.

"Darwin big and strong and brave," Rosita laughed sarcastically. He wouldn't let stupid things stop him from coming here. He's an educated man; he wouldn't let foolish people turn his head from you."

"Well, we shall see how it goes. He told me he saw a great big firefly the other night," Annette's voice was distant.

Rosita laughed loudly, then said, "Well, big men believing in a lotta rubbish."

Raynard sniggered.

"Thieves, rapists and drug addicts is plentiful in dis area. But you can find them all over de world. You just have to be careful. If people frighten to go out a their house, they'll never enjoy their life." Rosita Clements sucked her teeth.

"I suppose you're right; people have to be careful always whatever the circumstances and wherever they live," Annette was more assured.

"Girl, you have to be strong and brave in this world, for yourself and you son. Life hard but you have to fight it and win." Rosita smiled at Raynard.

Raynard smiled back. Raynard was very bright for his age. When his father left, it was as if he grew up overnight, if not in physique, certainly in mental prowess. Of late, he got tired quickly and had scratches on his body. The doctor suspected that he might be anaemic and prescribed medicine.

"That's true, Miss Clements," Annette was reflective. "We must all be brave and ready for anything. Life is full of ups and down, but as my mother used to say, life is sweet."

One evening, Annette and Darwin were caught up in each other's coos, moans, cravings and desires. They were sailing on a sea of passion, rubbing, kissing, feeling and caressing.

Darwin's mobile sang!

They came out of their enchantment and sat up suddenly.

Darwin felt for his mobile and answered, "Not now, please. I'll call you back, right."

Suddenly they heard dogs growling ferociously and fighting outside.

Then a cat wailed like a sick child.

They looked at each other questioningly.

"The environment is getting mess-up, thats why there are strange goings-on," Annette shrugged.

Darwin rose and went and looked out of a window.

"Can't see anything out there," he half whispered.

"It's only animals fighting over food or sex," smiled Annette.

Darwin was deep in thought.

Annette rose quickly, hugged him tightly and began kissing the back of his neck, his ears, then on the mouth.

The tongues in and around Ladbroke Grove clack-

clack ceaselessly about the gruesome events. In homes, shops, stores, supermarkets, on street corners, street-market stalls, building sites, cafes, pubs and offices.

- Oh, Gawd, what we go do!.....

- Me think is obeah......

- I blame it all on these foreigners....

- The drug dealers are making people insane.....

- Its them gang and them fightin'.....

- The price of property is bound to fall.....

- Somebody playing Dracula.....

- They should send for Buffy....

- Me 'fraid to walk 'bout in de night.....

- The devil on the loose around there....

- Don't let night catch you around here.....

- Its them terrorists......

- I'm moving to me sister's in Brixton......

- Oh, God, not my baby!....

- Listen, mate, it's black magic!.....

- Is it a bruise or a bite?.....

- First I thought it was a plane or a star....

- It's all this witchcraft on telly....

- Some people really sick.....

- What did you really see?....

- I couldn't believe me own eyes....

- I think it's UFO's.....

- The mind plays tricks all the time.....

- It could be for a sarcrifice....

- I armin meself, you hear!....

- I going to church everyday....

- They're bringing all their strange practices into this country....

Chapter six

It was a Sunday afternoon in March. Annette was at work and Darwin was looking after Raynard. He left Raynard watching television and went to Gawain's flat.

After knocking on the flat door and getting a "Come-in", he went in and found Gawain looking at designs of Carnival costumes. Gawain took months, sometimes years to prepare for a Carnival competition.

"Have a seat, man," Gawain smiled broadly, turning around to face Darwin.

Darwin took a seat in an armchair, his eyes roaming the pictures on the walls, tables and mantel-pieces.

"How are things with you?" Gawain was still smiling. "I'm alright, thank you," Darwin tried to relax, but something was on his mind. "You are always preparing for Carnival, aren't you!"

"Yes, I love it!" now Gawain's face was luminous with delight.

"Are you only interested in costumes of Caribbean images?" Darwin stood up and began walking around admiring the photographs and designs.

"I only do things from the Caribbean because I understand them more than European ones. I've been to the Caribbean several times recently and I've seen the Carnival there. And it always touches something deep inside me."

"I can understand that," Darwin's face was full of expression as he touched the designs and photographs. After long, careful thought, he said, "Do you know anything about the history or stories behind some of these figures in these costumes?" He was looking at two designs of folk mythological characters.

Gawain looked in Darwin's direction, "Oh, these, well, one is a folk character called, "a Soucouyant". And the other is my version of a kind of werewolf character called "a Lagahoo".

"Tell me about them," Darwin was holding the two designs as he sat back down in the armchair.

Gawain came to him and pointed to the design of the Lagahoo and said, "This one, yes. Mind you some people in the Caribbean believe these things are real. They say on full-moon nights, an old man turns into a huge dog and terrorises villages in the countryside. This old man deals with the Devil. There are many tales about "the Lagahoo." You can kill the Lagahoo with any weapon."

"Yes, it's like the werewolf legend in Europe, "Darwin sighed greatly. "French, I believe."

"The difference is, "Gawain went on. "There aren't any wolves in the Caribbean, so the old man turns into a big dog."

The design of the Lagahoo or "loup Garou", showed a ferocious looking Alsatian type dog with blood dripping from pointed, glistening teeth, wearing trousers cut below the knees and torn shirt. The eyes were bloodshot, fierce and piercing.

"And this other one. It's a female one, isn't it?" Darwin was a bit jovial.

The design of "the Soucouyant" showed an old woman with bloodshot eyes staring with open mouth showing pointed teeth, dressed in red, crimson and yellow ribbons, with her back exploding into a red, fiery satin. Her hair, wild, grey and unkempt, her arms, bony and long, showing claw-like fingers.

"Ah ha, thats one of my favourites, man," Gawain smiled. "I played that once in the Trinidad Carnival. I won second prize for best Individual costume. I'm thinking of playing it at the Carnival here in London." And he began to hum a calypso tune happily.

"This one is the Caribbean Vampire woman," Darvwin became very serious and it showed. "More superstition, eh!"

Gawain forced a smile and went on, "The Soucouyant legend, myth, call it whatever, is popular all over the Caribbean by different names. In Trinidad it's known as "Soucouyant"; in other islands it's known as "Old Higue," and in the French Caribbean island of Haiti, it's known as "Galipot." It's about an old woman who lives alone and is loved and respected in a village; she is always helpful with everything in the village. But in the night this loveable old woman, takes off her skin like a garment, hides it, turn into a blood-sucking monster, then flies out into the night as a ball of fire hunting for people's blood to suck. Sometimes, they say, the Soucouyant can turn into a firefly."

Darwin found the folk myths preposterous but then no more preposterous than the European Dracula legend. He began to piece it together in his mind: the ball of fire, the glowing insect or bird, the firefly, the victim drained of blood. Is there a link between this Caribbean mythology and what is going on in and around Ladbroke Grove? He didn't want people to think that he was mad. Nor did he want to become a laughing stock. He was going to be extra careful all the time.

"Is it always an old woman who turns into this blood-sucking killer?" he ventured.

"Yes, always. Nice mask, isn't it!"

"Yes, it's a nice costume. That's a fantastic image indeed, man. The Caribbean does have some extraordinary things," Darwin was cunning.

Gawain laughed heartily, "That's why I like costumes showing Caribbean things very much. I feel it's always the best." And he gaily went off to his small bathroom in a corner of the flat.

Gawain was a tailor, but most of the time he worked shift in a warehouse.

Darwin studied the design of the Soucouyant vampire. Could this be the evil that was terrorising that part of London? But it can't be. It's only superstition, folktale. Maybe some lunatic is going around imitating the behaviour of the Soucouyant?

Gawain came back and asked merrily, "Would you like something to drink, tea or something stronger?"

"No, thank you, nothing for me," And he persisted, "This Soucouyant character. Why does this old woman turn into this monster? For what purpose?"

Gawain carried on with what he was doing before the other man came to his flat. He now began to draw on a piece of mounting-board.

"Maybe it's an evil force or demon which disguises as an old woman," Gawain drew as he spoke. "Or maybe the old woman is doing it to get long life or wealth from the devil."

"Yes, I agree with you, it's fascinating," Darwin went on. "How long do they live? Can a Soucouyant be destroyed?"

"Yes, the legend says that first you must find out where she hides her skin and put salt on it. And what must also be done is lots and lots of raw rice grains must be sprinkled all around the area where her skin was hidden. The Soucouyant comes before morning to put on her skin and become the old woman once again. But she cannot touch her skin because it has salt on it. And she must count every rice grain before morning; when the morning sun catches her, she shrivels up and dies. Then the remains must be burned and put in a barrel of tar and thrown into the sea. And that's the end of the Soucouyant."Gawain grinned then laughed.

"Of course, it's impossible for her to count all the rice grains before morning, eh?" Darwin was deep in thought.

"Yes, she's trapped. She can't get away."

"It's great fairytales for children." Darwin smiled, "That's why Raynard like them so much."

Darwin rose and put the design of the Soucouyant character on a little table, stretched and said, "Well, I'd better go down and see how my little charge is doing."

Whenever he confronted Annette about the gruesome incidents in the area or anything relating to them, Darwin found that she wasn't interested or was sometimes angry.

"I've told you again and again," Annette would wave her arm about angrily. "I cant remember the stories my mother told me. Why should I remember them. They were told to me when I was a child. Now I'm a grown woman."

"Why do you get so angry!" Darwin asked calmly. "Because they're Caribbean stories. I'm living in England. I've no use whatsoever with Caribbean ways of life."

"Alright, dear, sorry to bother you with this" Darwin soothed.

Darwin spoke to several old people from the Caribbean, especially men, about Caribbean myths and superstition. Some were happy to speak about it; others resented it and got angry; these he suspected were hiding something or afraid of something or just downright ashamed of such superstition.

"Human beings are the strangest creatures on this earth," Darwin thought. "But I have to live with them."

He had made a appointment to see a West African teacher. He wanted to find out about African myths and superstition and their relation, if any to the gruesome incidents occurring in West London.

They met in a park on a bright and sunny spring Sunday in West Hampstead. He had known this teacher for some years; they were in and out of touch. The two men shook hands, laughed, then sat on a park bench.

"Hello, Darwin! It's been a long time!" greeted the teacher whose name was Olu, smiling.

"Yes, too long!" Darwin too was smiling, then sitting.

"How are things with you?" Olu asked still smiling. "Are you still with the old firm?"

"Yes, I'm still there. And you, are you still teaching?"

"Yes, but in a different school since a year ago."

"As I've said to you over the phone," Darwin began to lie. "I'm doing an evening class on African history and culture. It's very interesting. I like the mythology best of all."

Olu smiled and relaxed on the bench.

Pigeons and sparrows fluttered about. A soft spring breeze touched them with cool fingers. Children with adults entered the park happily.

"I'm particularly interested in mythological customs and the supernatural," Darwin pushed on.

"Well, there is magic, or as Europeans call it, "black magic." There is belief in evil spirits of the dead, evil demons, devils. There is also belief that human beings can turn into animals and prey on others."

"Do you mean like the European werewolf and vampire?" Darwin was unrelenting.

Olu was looking at a group of pigeons fussing over bits of bread.

"Not werewolves," Olu's brows knitted. "There aren't any wolves in Africa. Not where I come from anyway, not West Africa. But bats, yes, vampire ones."

"Do they suck the blood of their victims?"

Olu looked in the distance thoughtfully and said, "The superstition is, Vampires are evil spirits, and they are immortal. These vampires obtain a human body to live in; they keep close watch on a prospective victim whose body they wish to live in. In some African beliefs, souls of the dead, flutter about as bats. Ghosts in African stories eat people, carving them up. Vampires in Africa also use animal bodies to live in; animals such as crocodiles, hyena, leopard and lion.

In the Dracula-type of myth, there are sporadic traces of such beliefs both in Western, Southern, Central and Eastern Africa. A vampire-man can be recognised by his fang-like teeth and by his stench of death." Olu took a deep breath, looked around the park, and continued, "The Subaga of the Bammana tribe of Mali, are people who can leave their bodies and fly inside their victims' houses, then they pounce quietly on the victim and take his or her life."

Darwin was aware of the Slave Trade which must have taken myths and superstitions as well as people from Africa across the Atlantic to the tropical shores of the Caribbean. Some of the mythology struck him as simply out of this world. And he was mentally aroused and shaken.

"Does the legend say how these evil creatures can be killed or prevented?" He asked wearily.

"I can't remember much about that part of it," sighed Olu. "I think they can be burnt or beheaded."

"What about garlic, holy water and crucifixes as deterrents to keep them away from a victim?"

"No, I'm afraid not, they're not like the European ones. The wisemen of the tribe whom Europeans call witch-doctors, can get rid of these African demons."

"What about light or fire?" Darwin's face warmed. "Do these monsters give off any fire or light?"

"No, not at all."

Suddenly, the sky darkened as if the sunny spring day had put on a mask.

The two men arose together.

"It's just like English weather to be like this," Olu laughed. "Its going to rain, I bet."

"Nah, I don't think so," Darwin smiled.

Darwin didn't bring his car.

They shook hands, and the sun came out again.

"You see what I mean!" Olu smiled.

"Look, let's meet later for a drink and maybe a meal, eh?" Darwin was cheerful.

"That'll be great!" Olu beamed.

After his meeting with Olu, Darwin thought long and hard about everything and was now convinced that the monster whether human, animal or insect, had Caribbean connections. He spoke to old people from the Caribbean outside the area as far away as Brixton, and what they told him was the same as Gawain had told him.

He sometimes walked around the tormented area at night in summer, and was very clever at concealing this from Annette and others. He began to see old Caribbean women in a different light: they could be loving grandmothers, mothers and wives, but they could also be monsters in disguise.

Could it be that people from the Caribbean who have settled in England, didn't only bring their music , food, speech, dreadlocks hairstyle and Carnival, but also their supernatural practices? His imagination expanded.

Chapter Seven

The popular kerb-crawling street in Notting Hill, the haunt of prostitutes of every race, colour , age and price. The women paraded up and down the street which is always busy seven days, or rather seven nights a week.

The women wore anything to show off most of their bodies. In summer, they practically went about naked.

Late one summer's night, two young women who were very good friends, were standing in a dark alleyway which ran off the kerb-crawling street, when a tall man dressed in black approached them.

The man must have been about six feet tall, powerfully built and threatening. He was their pimp.

"Why you standing around here for!" he sneered at the two women. "You should be in the bright light selling your stuff. Remember, I don't intend to put up with that kinda pittance money you bring every night! I want some big money, not chicken-feed. Do you hear me, otherwise I'll put the two of you in hospital!"

The two women, frightened out of their skins, visibly shaking all over, answered together: "Yes, Singin, sorry, we're going."

"And remember, always use a condom. I don't want any women getting aids and dying and ruining the business. And no kissing the clients. If they want kissing, tell them to go to their wives!"

One of the women muttered something. Singin heard the sound but not what she actually said. He grabbed her by the neck swiftly with one arm and lifted her off the ground and growled, "What's your problem! You trying to say something, eh!"

The poor woman was unable to speak and was choking.

"She didn't mean anything, Singin. She was only clearing her throat. It's alright. We'll do what you say. After all, we're your best girls. Please, please, put her down!" pleaded the second woman.

Singin, looked at the other woman, then at the one he was holding, swayed her from side to side and was about to throw her down hard, when a huge ball of fire appeared over their heads, drawing nearer by the minute.

Singin completely terrified, released the woman who fell on her bottom. Singin's eyes popped out of his head, he couldn't speak; his blood froze, and he couldn't move from where he was standing.

The two women, looking up, choked, trying to speak, trying to scream.

Then swiftly the ball of fire swooped down onto Singin's head and severed it from the body. It ripped the stomach open, gulped blood, then it severed Singin's genitals and threw them away over the rooftops.

The two woman made out a skinless, bat-like thing attached to the ball of fire. Its blood red eyes stared at them, then it flew away over the rooftops. The two women held onto each other, wet themselves and shook violently with total horror.

Singin was ebony in complexion, his skin now turned pale pink, his head rolled like a football between the two horrified women. Then their voices returned. They bawled for help! Screamed blue murder! And pretty soon, the scene was filled with people, police and an ambulance.

The police questioned the women, and were convinced that they had killed the pimp. The two women, crying and still terrified, were taken away by the police.

Singin's body and head were taken away by the ambulance.

Other prostitutes were convinced that Singin was killed because he was known for his brutality.

There were people who said that it was the work of the blood sucking demon who only attacked wicked people and criminals.

Other people thought that aliens from outer space were killing people in the area.

The residents wanted the authorities to clear the area of prostitutes, pimps and drug pushers. But the prostitutes were very clever and tactful in picking up their clients.

More and more police patrolled all over Ladbroke

Grove, stopped and searched any strange or suspicious person.

When Darwin heard the news, he was sure that it was his quarry. He roamed the area where Singin was killed. His plan was to question the two prostitutes who had witnessed the crime. He spoke to them after they left the station.

The two women were still distraught and frightened. One was slim, blonde and in her twenties. The other, older, late thirties or early forties, a red-head and plump.

Darwin was patient.

"I still can't believe what I saw...the....if...I...!" the blond one broke down, shaking all over.

"How many times must we say that," the older woman was tired. "It was a ball of light. It looked as if somebody was wearing it. I don't know. It was a hideous face with snarling red mouth with sharp long teeth. I know Singin was a wicked bully, but it was a horrible way to die."

"This light was a ball of fire, yes," Darwin tried to sound less interrogative. "I believe you saw what you said you saw.

They stared at Darwin in wonderment.

"I know you didn't murder, and couldn't murder this Singin," Darwin's voice was extremely soothing.

"The others think we murdered him," the slim blonde stuttered. "But it was that thing in the bright light, sir," and she broke down again.

"It was flying over the houses," put in the older woman. "We're telling the truth, sir. We didn't kill nobody."

"I wonder what was it...it...it can't be...true...it... people talk about a monster in this place, but...I..." said the blonde and broke down again.

"I understand what you are saying, I assure you," Darwin forced a smile. "Do you live in Notting Hill?"

"Yes, we share a flat together," answered the red-head.

"Maybe another pimp who wanted to move in on Singin's territory, killed him. But...but...in that...way.... why." the slim one managed to splutter.

"And then it could be other women who wanted

him dead," the red-head was thoughtful.

Darwin was only interested in the blood-sucking aspect of the matter.

"Singin harassed the women, demanded more and more money from them. So I suppose everybody hated him and wanted him out of the way, even if it meant killing him," the red-head went on.

The two prostitutes didn't know what to believe; they didn't want to believe their own eyes. They were in total confusion.

"Yes, it is a horrible way to die," Darwin was careful to sift his thoughts before expressing them. " The person who did the killing must have tremendous strength, or they used a weapon like a sword or machete. This Singin was a massive man."

"And it flew away like a bird over the rooftops," the slim blonde whimpered. "It was some kinda monster maybe."

"And it was drinking his blood," the red-head put in. "The police said it drank all his blood. Some people does believe and do some weird things in this world."

"It could've been anything or anyone, sir," the slim, blonde yawned in between her words.

Darwin was satisfied that the two women had nothing to do with Singin's death. He studied the women carefully;they were only prostitutes, nothing more; they were not only afraid but hungry looking. He looked into the night sky which was grey and murky suggesting rain. A moon sulked through the clouds but stars twinkled. He stood for a while, thinking, then walked slowly, continuing his vigil.

In a side street, a cul-de-sac, a young man in his late teens squatted; he was shaking all over. He had a syringe in one hand and was slapping veins in the other arm, mumbling, "Come on, stand up for me! Damn it, I can hardly see it!" He lit a cigarette-lighter. His veins were punctured and sore.

Darwin came to the side street and heard it, he thought that it was a prostitute and a client. He stopped instantly, turned and went into the cul-de-sac which was a hemmed in by the back and sides of shops and a park with a high wall. As he came forward he saw the trembling young man in the faint glimmer of the cigarette lighter.

The young man got frantic as Darwin approached; he tried to rise but his legs failed him. He tried to speak, but his voice also failed him.

Suddenly a blinding flash of light from a ball of fire in the sky above them, lit up the place. It blinded Darwin for a while and he held up his hands to cover his eyes.

There was a scream of anguish, then the fire-ball disappeared. Darwin looked about him wildly, then gathered his composure.

The cigarette lighter was still on. When he came near to it, he gasped in horror; for the young man was lying there with utter horror masking his face which was white as a sheet and contorted beyond description. He was still trembling, his body was half-white/half-black and he was vomiting. He wasn't bitten. Darwin bent down and examined the whole area with his small flashlight, down to the smallest detail; then he rang for an ambulance. As he was being carried away, the young man was raving madly.

Darwin stood for a long while, and muttered, "Well,

Singin's women were certainly right."

Rain began to fall, it poured down, and went on and on until early the next day.

Chapter Eight

The Police stepped up their efforts: more and more police patrolled Ladborke Grove and the surrounding areas. The Commissioner went on television, assuring the public that things were under control, that the area was under heavy surveillance night and day.

Around midnight, in late June, the Soucouyant as a firefly circled the rooftops and surveyed the surroundings; it spied a woman waiting at a bus stop for the night bus, swooped down and hovered about five feet over her.

The woman, young and frightened out of her skin, stuttered, "What's this! What are you playing at! Is this some kind of helicopter joke! But you're a small light. What! A glider shining a flashlight in people's faces! You want to attack me! You're that......!"

The firefly came at the woman who began to scream, but no one came to her aid. She began to run, ducking into alleyways and side streets. But the flaming firefly was always above. Finally, she was cornered in a dark alleyway.

"Don't play the fool, whoever you are! Leave me alone! Help! Help! Somebody help me! Where is the police?!" The woman wailed and panted profusely, leaning against a wall.

The firefly's flame swelled into a huge ball of fire, from the fire an old woman came towards her. The frightened young woman felt safe at last, and with great relief, said, "Oh, thank God, some one is with me....I.....I...... thought......I.....was the only one about. It was like a helicopter flashlight chasing me, but it had wings. At first I thought it was some kind of a handglider playing the fool. I don't think it was. Some people do the silliest things for fun these days. It's good to see somebody else in the streets. You came just in time."

Before her baffled disbelieving eyes, the old woman changed into a skin-less, red-eyed, long grey haired demon with fire flowing in her bottom. Her mouth snarled with long teeth and blood dripping. Her eyes were wild and in a frenzy.

The frightened young woman's face ached in terror; her eyes became watery, then bloodshot; there was loud ringing in her ears, her hair stood on end and her skin became prickly, then changed from pink to dark brown. She began to vomit broke wind and diarrhoed. The sky suddenly became dark, ominous and overcast. The young woman's stomach ached as claw-like fingers gripped it and tore. Then the snarling mouth sucked, draining the blood from the body. The young woman's final expression was a whimper: "Where's the police!" Then her body shook, then became still.

Most of the national newspapers ignored what was going on in the Ladbroke Grove area, they had already stereotyped the area as a place of all kinds of criminality.

The streets remained deserted at night.

On a hot midnight in June in a maisonette of two floors. A husband and wife in their mid-fifties were on the second floor which was of three bedrooms and a bathroom, arguing. The couple had a history of domestic violence. They were married in their early twenties and had two children who were now teenagers and had left home. The man was big and tall, towering over the woman who was small. The violence always began with an argument, sometimes a silly argument, always started and pursued by the man.

"You're so bloody stupid!" the man pouted. "Your brain is so tiny that's why you can't understand it!"

"But that's not what I meant," the woman's voice was soft and trembling.

"I don't think you ever know what you mean!" the man's voice was beginning to storm.

"Please don't tell me you know what's in my mind," the woman dared. "You think you know everything, that's your trouble. Maybe your brain is smaller than mine!"

"The children would agree with me!" the man ventured. "They're intelligent. They've got my genes alright!"

"You live in a world of your own, don't you!" the woman knew she was on a dangerous ground but she couldn't stop herself. "They couldn't stand your selfish dictatorial behaviour. That's why they left when they did!" She certainly touched a raw nerve.

The man spun around in a flash of temper, seized the woman by the throat and began to choke her.

"Don't you dare put my kids against me, you fucking cunt!" The man was now fuming.

The woman was gasping for breath, waving her arms wildly as the man choked her with both hands.

"You piece of shit! You've been taking my children away from me! You cruel bastard!"

The woman struggled and struggled, arms flying, legs kicking, body convulsed.

"I'll squeeze the living crap out of you!" the man's face became pure fury. "I don't know why the fuck I married you. I must have been out of my mind. One of these days I'm going to end your useless life!"

The woman tried and tried to free herself but couldn't as she was being held in a steel–like grip of maddened rage. She passed out and became limp in his hands. Then she began to groan, then wail.

The man released his hold. And the woman fell over onto the carpeted floor.

The wail came again! But it didn't come from the woman's crumpled body on the floor. It seemed to come from outside the window.

The man looked around the room quizzically, then at the window, went and opened it. A hot wind met his face as he looked out into the night. A ball of fire knocked his head back and he staggered into the room. Then it came into the room, glowing brightly, swirling around the man with sucking and slurping sounds coming from it.

"Are you going to kill her" a voice from the swirling bright fire ball blurted out. "You big good for nothing bully!"

The man began to drip with sweat and fear. His eyes swelled and his huge frame shook like a leaf. He held his head with both hands and began to cry like a child, "Oh, oh.....it's....it's...the...the..the...thing...the monster... Where's my garlic! Where's my crucifix!" he fumbled in his trouser-pocket and took out a silver cross about two inches long which fell from his trembling fingers. And to the crumpled body of his wife, he commanded roughly, "Get up and get the holy water! You lazy cow! Why are you lying there like that! You're not dead! Get up, you bitch! The monster is going to kill us! Get up, wretch! Get up, quick!"

The crumpled body didn't stir.

"Oh, Almighty God, save me!" he stuttered. "It's true. There's a demon in the area killing innocent people." His heart drummed like a million drums.

"I don't know what she sees in you!" the voice from the swirling, slurping, sucking fireball roared. "You bloody bastard, I wouldn't even take you blood. I'm only going to end your worthless life!" And it pounced on his neck and throat and tore out his throat. Then it ripped off his trousers and underwear, tore off his penis and testicles and stuffed them in his mouth. The man's body kept twitching and shaking in a pool of blood on the floor.

The ball of fire swirled around the room once more then shot out of the window and into the night.

A young man and woman were making love in a

park on a very hot night in early July. The sky was blue and bright with stars. A half moon peeped through whiffs of white clouds.

"Its great doing it under the stars," cooed the young woman. "It's like we're born again."

"Yes, my darling," the young man sang as he kissed her nose, ears, eyes, neck and lips. "I want to do it everywhere with you."

"That's what we'll do," the young woman laughed. "We'll fuck everyewhere and at anytime. We love each other and the world should know."

They were both completely naked.

The man was on top of the young woman. They rolled over and she was on top of him. The stars seemed to twinkle in her eyes and she became mischievous.

"We can be like those streakers," she was now laughing uncontrollably. "Imagine instead of watching their football team, they'll be watching us, we'll be the centre of attraction, the celebrities. We'll be the stars of the nation's sports grounds." And she rode his penis to ecstasy.

"Oh, God, I'm coming....sweet....heart!" the young man began to explode inside her.

She sucked his breasts, held her own breasts and panted, "Not before me! Oh, oh, oh, oh, oh, we're coming together! The fuck is soooooo...sweeeet! We're in heaven.....Oh, God, I'm coming!"

Only the half moon and stars were witnesses to this sweet love-making. So they thought.

Suddenly! A ball of fire appeared and swirled around them.

The young couple with stars in their eyes and love-sweetness in their hearts, thought the ball of fire was a shooting star. They laughed and said, "Look!" it was as if they were under a spell with the sweetness of love-making.

"Oh God, it's so beautiful," the young woman moaned.

Their faces mirrored the brightness of the ball of fire. Then the young man reached and tried to tough the swirling ball of fire which stopped swirling and a voice came from it, "Nah! Don't touch me, you bastard! Touch this filthy bitch who's on heat like an animal in the jungle! But never touch me, you hear!"

The young couple, dumbfounded, sat up and stared, their faces now stricken with shock and fear. The young man sprang to his feet and helped his partner up.

Let's go quickly!" he said, gathering up their clothes. "It's that.....that...thing...you know! Come on! It's that... fiery blood sucking bird thing! Come on, hurry!"

"But....but...it....it's talk....talking.....how does....it... it," the young woman scooped up some of her clothing.

They tried to run off, but the ball of fire knocked them onto the ground. All the sexual joy had gone from them; they now feared for their lives. The young man was knocked over onto his back and he lay flat out. The young woman was knocked onto her stomach; she was shrieking, "Whatever you are, please leave us alone!"

"Fuck you!" the voice from the ball of fire shouted. And as it swirled over the young man's face, there was a snarl. Then the ball of fire covered the young man's face and tore out his throat.

"Leave him alone!" the young woman screamed. "Help! Somebody help us!" She jumped and went to the aid of her boyfriend.

The ball of fire shot at her head, knocking her unconscious on the ground. Then it returned to the young man and sucked his blood, almost draining the body. It then bit off his penis and spat it on the ground.

Then it flew to the young woman's unconscious body and muttered, "You're too damn stupid!" And it ripped out her guts and drank her blood.

A man had stalked a woman for months; he was besotted with her. He knew where she lived and worked. He had taken photographs of her which adorned the bedroom of his council flat like a shrine. Sometimes he stripped himself naked in his bedroom and masturbated as he looked at the photographs of her. This went on for months until he could bear it no longer. He wanted her in flesh; he wanted to touch her, to feel her body against his. He imagined her body warm and intoxicating.

He continued to stalk her and waited for the moment when she would be all alone, then he would make his move.

His moment came one Friday night. She was hurrying home, she had worked late, and he waited outside her workplace since late afternoon.

It was a cool late May night.

She took a shortcut through an alleyway. Perfect, he thought. He kept a safe distance behind her. But as he came to the alleyway, she had disappeared. He ran to the end of the alleyway, looked around, frantic, but didn't see her. If she came out of the alleyway, where was she? How could she have moved that fast? She couldn't have disappeared into thin air! Then he heard a sound in the alleyway. He ran to the alleyway, and saw her coming towards him. But? How? He couldn't understand it. He smiled as he approached her.

"You shouldn't be out in the night by yourself." He beamed. "It'd dangerous, you know!"

With those words she felt threatened, she frowned, continued walking and said, "Thanks for caring about me but I'm alright, really I am."

The man felt rejected and he couldn't take that.

He grabbed her arm and said, "Don't go away from me. Let's talk! Let me keep you company until you get to your house, please!"

"How dare you touch me?" the woman snapped and pulled her arm away. I don't know you! You think you own me!"

The man insisted and grabbed her around the waist. She pushed him off and he fell over. Then she disappeared again.

"Where! What! She has disappeared again! How does she do that! Well, I don't care. I'm going to have you tonight whether you want to or not. Come here! You know you want it as much as me!" His heart was beating, his penis rose hard as steel.

Suddenly, the sky became very dark, the surroundings were also dark. A little light came out of the darkness, then it grew into a fire ball and a voice spoke from it, "So you're going rape me eh! Come on then!" Then the fireball darted around, up and down, then around the man. "Oh, I cant see! Where!" the man yelped. "Oh, God, don't kill me! Help!"

In the darkness there were snorts, snarls, grunts, growls, groans, bawling and the sound of sucking and slurping as the man's stomach was being torn open, his entrails scattered everywhere. His penis and testicles were put in his stomach, and his body was drained of blood.

Chapter Nine

In the height of the summer in July, Annette was in full bloom in her love for Darwin. Raynard liked Darwin a lot as well, and always kept out of their way when he suspected that they wanted to be alone. Raynard was soon to be at secondary school.

One Friday night, Raynard was fast asleep after staying up late watching television.

Annette and Darwin began to kiss passionately. The television was on, they took no notice of it. "Let's go in the bedroom," Annette whispered but didn't move.

Darwin didn't move either.

They were lost in each other's sweetness and love play.

A dog howled outside, it sounded like it was

coming from outside their door. It raged on and on as if it was trying to come into the building, or was barking at an intruder. Suddenly a bright light emanated from the street.

Then Annette began to pull at Darwin's clothes, to get them off. He, in turn, began to undress her.

The dog raged on and on.

Annette and Darwin were now half-naked. Annette kept whispering, "Let's go in the bedroom," but wasn't getting up from the floor where they were lying, loving each other to the limits.

The dog stopped growling.

The bright light went out in the street.

Annette and Darwin were panting heavily. They rolled over onto their backs, sweating and panting heavily. Annette threw her arms around him and said, "Let's go in the bedroom."

They went into the bedroom. And until later on in the morning, they made love in every position possible.

"Good Morning!" Rosita Clements sang with a slight knock on their door.

Darwin came into the sitting room area from the bathroom. Darwin and Annette looked at each other, they weren't ready to receive guests as yet. They didn't respond to the greeting and kept quiet.

Then they heard with a great relief as Rosita called out, "Alright, if you're not up yet, I'll let you rest. I go come back later!"

Later when she came back, Darwin had already left. "You know, girl, I see a firefly outside me window de other night late" Rosita said in a dreamy way. "I think it's de heat does bring out some strange things in this country."

"I agree with you, "Annette sighed. "These hot summers and mild winters we've been having aren't meant to be. England is becoming like the tropics."

"There's a lotta sense in dat, girl," Rosita said darkly. "Sometimes I does feel weak and tired. And I have like mosquito bites on me belly. Yes, de summer heat stifling people."

"I've noticed those bites on Raynard as well. I think I told you about it."

You must rub ointment on it, girl," Rosita soothed. "And you must be very watchful all de time."

Annette was too absorbed in her own personal life and plans to worry unduly about the strange gruesome incidents that were occurring in and around Ladbroke Grove.

Annette and Darwin became deeply involved. Many times Annette would spend nights at Darwin's place. Then her landlady or Gawain would look after Raynard. Sometimes Annette made other arrangements with Jocelyn.

Annette was becoming quarrelsome, picking on Raynard for the slightest thing.

Raynard too, was always tired and grumpy.

"Don't be too hard on de boy," Rosita said to Annette one morning. "Whatever problem you having, it's not he fault. I does hear you giving 'im a hard time. If you keep on like dat, he going to grow to hate you."

Raynard was in the bedroom.

Annette played with the scrambled eggs, bacon and toast.

One night, Rosita was telling stories to Raynard in her flat. He interrupted her and said in a voice of regret and longing, "Miss Clements, I'd love to hear a story about......" And here he broke off because he had forgotten the name of the mythology or legend. "What is it called.....I can't remember... its about a....let me..... now,,,,,, it's called a.......a.....a....a"

Rosita didn't indulge in his guessing game. Then it came to him.

"Yes, yes, I remember now, yes," he smiled. It's about something called a....a...a..a suckiyan, yes....yes.. it's like a vampire, sucking people's blood in the night, yes. Tell me a story like that. My granny used to tell me stories about it."

Rosita remembered such stories of her childhood in the Caribbean. She searched her memory for the one Raynard mentioned.

"After all dat's happening around this area, you not frighten," she said sternly.

"I'll be afraid because you're such a great storyteller but I'll get over it, because it's not true. I remember more:

Its about a woman who turns into the thing called a Soucouyant, and flies about in the night sucking people's blood. That's for sure. Please. Please, tell me a story about that," Raynard pleaded excitedly.

Rosita was in deep thought, then said, "I don't know lotta stories about such a thing. You granny did know more about it than me. It's fairytale. Some people in de Caribbean does tell children dem stories to frighten dem, to stop dem from beheaving bad. Me don't want to make you have bad dreams, boy."

Raynard sulked; he was disappointed; he thought Rosita knew all the stories from the Caribbean, or most of them. His childhood imagination and expectancy were greater than ever. "But you're a great storyteller, better than my granny was. I thought you knew millions of tales from over there."

Rosita laughed. "Thank you, boy. I know a few, and I did tell you about dem already. You forget. I go tell you a nice story about de trickster, Anancy, the Spider-man. It is not scary. You mother tell me you does get too frighten."

"I'm tired of hearing about Anancy, Miss Rosie, "

Raynard yawned.

"You want to go to you bed, then, you sleepy?"

"No, no, no yet. I'm not going to get scared, I promise."

Rosita began the story.

Raynard fell asleep on Rosita's settee. When he awoke he was in his bed. His mother was bending over him, saying, " Have a nice sleep, darling?"

Jocelyn had strange dreams, sometimes the dreams ended in nightmares. The dreams ended with her flat on fire and she trapped in it.

At first, she saw a light by a window, then she heard a knocking on her flat door, a knocking that turned into banging, then a voice calling to her. "Joyce! Come quick! Let me out! Save me! The house is on fire!"

One night she was lying on her bed and couldn't sleep. She had been having sleepless nights with terrible headaches for some time now. Her doctor had prescribed sleeping pills and lots of rest. But she couldn't relax. Her flat became pitch-black, then a light like a firefly's appeared in the room. She tried to get up but couldn't;

she tried to speak, but her voice didn't obey her. She couldn't move her body; she could only see and smell. Her flat smelt of incense.

The light from the firefly grew bigger, and then it hovered over, brighter and brighter it became. She tried desperately to move but couldn't. Thoughts raced through her mind: "This is the blood-sucker! It's going to kill me drink my blood! Oh, God I don't want to die! God, Help me! I.....I....but I don't understand....I....how come...I'm...."

Then a voice from the firefly's light filled the room. "I can be anything you want me to be! Sweet Joyce! Darling Jocelyn! What do you want from me?" It was an unearthly voice.

Then the room cleared! It was morning. She was having a nightmare. She woke with a great start, sprang from the bed and rushed around the flat crazily, muttering, "Leave me alone." Then she sat on a chair and collected herself.

Chapter Ten

Darwin thought that the vampire or "Soucouyant," didn't go out every night. He thought the monster had changed habits because it was now operating in the new surroundings of England. Also it changed habits to ward off suspicions. And he began to suspect Rosita Clements, but kept it to himself for now. People can live very secret lives; you think you know them but you don't. He thought Rosita's basement was like a kind of hell; the curtains were never drawn to let in fresh air or sunshine, and the place smelt mouldly.

One night, at the end of spring, there was a commotion at one end of a street where he roamed. He rushed to the scene, and made out that it was a crowd of about sixty people and two policemen. Two women had seen, what they thought was a UFO hovering over their homes nearby. One of the women, in her sixties, was completely distraught.

"I never believe in such things, you understand," she stammered, trembling and swaying, while a young woman tried to steady her. "I thought that I was dreaming. Maybe I was dreaming...this is fantastic.!"

The younger woman comforted and wiped the older woman's brow and said, "We were coming home after visiting a friend who was poorly; when I saw it. I thought it was a plane. I rubbed my eyes. I couldn't believe it. It.....it.....it....was a huge....oval shape with lights all around the side. And.....as it flew over, it let out a glowing light on the building as if it was trying get a better look at everything, I don't know. Then suddenly, it just shot off or disappeared.....I can't say for sure ....I.....I...."

"Come, come, ladies and gentlemen, clear the street!" called a policeman. "Go back to your homes! It's nothing to be alarmed about!"

"Nothing to be alarmed about! I ask you!" stuttered the older woman.

"Are you two drunk!" jeered a tall young man.

"You've been watching too much X Files and Star Trek!" and he started off.

"You stupid fool! You're the one who's drunk on drugs. We know what we saw!" the younger woman raged.

"Now, now, calm, down, madam!" the policeman cautioned.

The crowd was breaking up. The street was beginning to clear.

Darwin was utterly disappointed. Although he had an open mind, his concerns about phenomena were only of this earth at the present time. He went to the two women and said, "Goodnight, ladies. I'm very interested in what you saw." He was shrewd and diplomatic. "But was it the first time you saw this spacecraft?"

The two women felt relieved and satisfied that at last someone believed them. They thought they were going mad when they saw the flying object; they thought that they were having hallucinations. They eyed Darwin from head to feet. Then the younger woman breathed a sigh of relief and replied, "Yes, it was the first time we saw anything like that. That's the honest truth."

"I swear it's the truth. It was the first time, yes," the older woman seemed to moan. "I know people will think it's all in our minds, but we truelly did see it," then she broke down crying.

The younger woman embraced her and said softly, "Don't cry, Auntie, it's alright."

"Did you see any aliens?" Darwin went along with their story. "If so, what did they look like?"

"No, no, just the spaceship with lights, just lights. We didn't see anything else," answered the younger woman. "And it vanished so fast like it was never there!"

"I see, hummmmm," Darwin nodded thoughfully. "What's the matter, you don't believe us as well! the older woman snapped. "Why are you pulling such a funny face?"

"I believe you, of course I do," Darwin forced a wide smile. "I have heard it all before."

"I think these things are true and the government and the authorities are hiding it from the people," the older woman who was frightened said. "I used to say that things and life from outer space was all nonsense and idle talk. But now I've seen with my own eyes. I know it now for a fact. I believe it all with my heart and soul".

"And you're not alone, dear," chirped her niece. The crowd had cleared. Only the two women and Darwin were on the scene.

"Have you heard about the incidents of people being sucked by some kind of bat or dog?" Darwin was getting weary; he thought the two women saw the blood-sucking demon but mixed it up with a UFO sighting, maybe they had confused what they saw with programmes on television. He looked around; the sky was grey, the moon was low, it was very late.

"Yes, we've heard about that," stuttered the two women together.

"We think that's somebody gone crazy on drugs," said the younger woman.

"Do you think that someone could be attacking people and sucking their blood if they weren't on drugs?" the older woman gasped for air.

Darwin thought that most people would have thought the same about the two women, that they were hallucinating on some kind of drug, or that they were drunk. "Thank you, ladies. Goodnight," and he went off.

He walked around the area until early morning, saw nothing suspicious, felt tired and awkward, then he went home.

The day broke open wide with the terrible news that a baby in the same area, was killed; the infant's stomach torn apart and its blood drained. The head was severed from the body and it's genitals were bitten off and stuffed up its rectum. It was a male white boy whose skin turned completely black and its eyes popped out its head. Some police women and men were sick, it was rumoured that someone vomited blood.

Darwin was horrified and racked his brain for an explanation. He worked overtime for a solution. He even went to the British Museum and read up about primitive tribes who ate their dead to get strength, intelligence, power and any other skill they possessed when they were alive. Also about blood sacrifice and ancestor worship.

And he read everything he could about vampirism and lycanthropy. His mind wandered onto Rosita Clements. Her face, sometimes youthful and smiling, sometimes lined and haggard. Her arms, strong with muscles like a man's, her chest, also like a man's, flat. How old was she? Not much is known about her. She has no family and friends. Maybe she is a devil-worshipper? Maybe she is the Soucouyant? Maybe she was cursed, she can't help it! There was something about her which overwhelmed him.

The following night late, he patrolled the area where the male white baby was killed. A man approached him and asked for a light for his cigarette, he obliged. Although Darwin didn't smoke, he always carried matches nowadays for any emergency.

The sky darkened and scowled into rain. Darwin walked quickly to shelter. When the rain ceased, he went home.

The rain returned and fell all night. There was a crack of thunder and then a streak of lightning which lit up the whole of Ladbroke Grove and Notting Hill like broad daylight. The weather raged on and on.

Darwin fell asleep as he hit the bed because he was dead tired.

Chapter Eleven

Darwin was thinking of marrying Annette. He was making plans. He thought about buying a house; he had savings and thought about getting a loan from a Building Society. He was determined to do everything to make Annette happy.

Raynard was very happy, he liked Darwin and wanted a Dad.

Rosita Clements was happy for Annette. "You was always a good tenant. No trouble at all. I always treat you like family, because you mother and father come from my part of de world. I hope everything work out for you and you son."

"You know, Miss Clements, all the experiences I've had with men have taught me many things which are always going to be very helpful. I think Darwin is going to be different," Annette smiled and looked away.

On a hot, sizzling summer's night in late June, Darwin came home very late. His flat was a one-bedroomed dwelling in a three storyed building. It had been a day of unbearable heat; most people commented on it.

But vampire Soucouyant was in its elements.

Darwin sprawled himself on a sofa, before getting up and chilling himself out with a cold beer. He sat for a long while, sipping and comtemplating the grey carpeted floor. He drained the can, changed into a flowery, satin dressing gown and muttered, "Soon, I'll have a lovely woman to come home to. Someone to look after me." He smiled contentedly and went into the shower. He sang happily, laughed and said, "And soon I'll solve this mystery of this blood-sucking monster and get rid of the perpetrator."

Darwin and Gawain became very good friends. Over lunch on a Saturday at Annette's flat, Darwin, Gawain and Annette were talking about the coming Carnival, when Darwin suddenly changed the subject. Raynard was in his room with friends.

"What do you know about that Rosita Clements woman?" Darwin said gravely.

Annette looked completely shaken.

Gawain was ill at ease.

"She's...she's...just.....just...an old woman living by herself. I've told you before, she's very kind to me and Raynard. What's there to know about her. But I've told you this before." The words seemed to come out of Annette's mouth without her control.

"She treats me very well," Gawain cut in. "I've no complaints. Sometimes she cooks and offers me some."

"Yes, I must say, I find her very welcoming," Darwin said thoughtfully.

"What...what... are you getting at?" Annette eyes were narrow and remote.

"She doesn't seem to have anybody, don't you find that strange?" Darwin had a puzzled look.

"Not in this country, man!" Gawain laughed. "I mean people can live as neighbours for donkey years, and they don't know each other. They don't even say, "Good Morning" or "Hello". When one of them dies, it's the

Social Services people who discover them."

"I know all that, Arthur, but English people do have visitors, even if it's an only friend." Darwin was defiant.

Annette looked at him and her face showed pain.

But you don't know who comes to see her when we're not here, do you?" Gawain sounded triumphant.

"And why do they come here when we're not here!" Darwin carried on regardless.

"Well, that's her business, isn't it, not ours!" Annette tried to be jovial.

"I can't understand all the secrecy," and Darwin looked away. "Is she hiding something?" he ventured.

"A old woman like dat can't be hiding nothing, man!" Gawain broke into Caribbean language, achieving a smile from Darwin and even Annette.

"You're right," Darwin said, still smiling and looking at Annette. " It's not our business." And he ploughed into his food.

Annette too was still smiling as she said, "Come on, eat up!" She had prepared fried chicken, chips, peas and a salad.

"Nice salad, Annette," beamed Gawain as he helped himself to a second helping. And now it was Gawain's turn to change the subject.

"I was thinking," he began seriously. "How about making it a foursome. We can go to see a show or a film in the West End, then meal afterwards?"

"What do you mean, foursome!" Darwin looked at him and then at Annette. "There are only three of us here!"

"Well, I....I...was thinking, maybe we could ask Jocelyn to come with us."

"You.....you...mean....you want to...!" Darwin giggled, food flew from his mouth.

"Yes, that's a great idea, Arthur!" Annette said brightly. "I'll tell her. I'm sure she'll love to come with us."

Gawain belched and nodded.

Whenever Jocelyn came to visit Annette she always left before night.

On a Sunday, Jocelyn visited Annette. Jocelyn reclined on the sofa.

Raynard was in his room playing with a video

game.

"Ann, I feel so strange sometimes," Jocelyn said dreamily. "Maybe I'm going out of my head."

"No, no, don't talk like that," Annette was petulant. "It's how Ricky died, that's what still on your mind."

"It's not that," Jocelyn's voice became tearful.

"I've been having some nasty nightmares. And they're so real sometimes. At times I feel I walk in my sleep."

"It's understandable after what you've been through," Annette forced a wide smile.

"One morning I woke up and found dirt, grass and spots of blood all over my nightie," as Jocelyn spoke she shuddered.

"That's from your period," Annette cuddled her friend. "You were having a bad period in your nightmares, that's all. You need lots of rest, girl. Your body needs building up. Don't worry about nonsense. I know there are nasty things going on around here, but all that is just blown up out of proportion by the newspapers and silly people. You know, Gawain wants the four us;

Darwin and me, and you and him to go for a night out in the West End. What do you think of that, eh?"

After giving the matter some thought, Jocelyn responded, "That sounds alright. I'd like that, yes. The four of us will be fine."

Annette smiled, "You must give yourself a good time, enjoy life. Life's too short to spend it worrying about rubbish."

"You're right, I suppose."

"Of course, I'm right!" Annette sparkled. " Would you like an egg-nog?"

"Yes, please, that would be nice," and Jocelyn sighed heavily. Annette laughingly went to the kitchen.

It became clear to Darwin that Gawain was in love with Jocelyn, in fact, he was consumed with love for her. Whenever her name was mentioned Gawain's face lit up. And Darwin also noticed that whenever Gawain saw her, his movements became confused and awkward, and his speech became tongue-tied or in stutters. He tried to control himself but he was too weak with deep feelings for her. He tried to be tactful but words, phrases, gestures and looks, gave him away. Darwin sensed an electric current running through the two of them whenever they were in each other's company. Darwin picked up all their shocks and vibrations. Whenever the three of them were together, Darwin always made some kind of excuse to leave them alone together.

Old Eddy, a vagrant who lives in the street, begs for money and cigarettes, was found dead, his throat was torn out and his body drained of blood.

At first the police thought that Eddy's death was the result of how he lived, that he most likely picked up a disease from the street. He did have a habit of searching in litter-bins and other rubbish.

They thought that his torn-out throat and loss of blood, were coincidences.

Voices in the street gave opinions:

- Poor Eddy, what a horrid way to go.....
- Eddy musta eat some kinda poison, man....
- Well, so you live, so you die. I mean living in dustbins....
- He must have suffered a lot.....

- Death comes like thief in de night....

- It's de hot weather; it does bring out dem blood sucking insect.....

- It's the same thing that bit those other people, bit poor old Eddy.....

- My Nan said it's like Jack the Ripper....

- Me don't go out in de night at all...

- I does burn incense to keep away those evil spirits....

- It's the way the environment has been messed up.....

- They experiment on animals and sometimes it goes wrong.....

- De world in a·mess, man.....

- It's a mad murderer who thinks he is Dracula....

- De streets dirty and stink, de council don't clean it....

- I think its aliens from another world.....

- Poor man, rest in peace, Eddy.....

Mrs Cherry, a Primary School-teacher at Raynard's

school sent a message via Raynard to Gawain for him to come to the school to give a talk to the children on Carnival.

Mrs Cherry lived about two or three streets from Rosita Clements' house. She too lived alone.

Mrs Cherry encouraged multicultural education at the school by various speakers, storytellers and musicians from various ethnic groups. She thought it was essential that children of whatever ethnic origin know about the culture and life of their parents or grandparents.

Gawain and Darwin were at Annette's flat one night when Darwin was baby-sitting Raynard. Raynard had been watching television, but afterwards, he went to bed. The two men discussed the matter. Darwin turned off the television.

"It's not the first time she has asked me," Gawain relaxed on the sofa, sipping a cup of cocoa.

"I've heard that there are many English people like her," Darwin too was drinking cocoa; he was sitting on a chair.

"I think it's very important," Gawains voice was

forceful. "It's gives children solid confidence."

"I agree. Annette doesn't seem to think so."

"Well, I suppose because she was born here," Gawain was thoughtful. "I don't think she has ever been to the Caribbean, or had any real association with it."

"She's not the only one," Darwin's face was sprinkled with light and shadow. "I know people who don't even want to talk about the Caribbean, sometimes they even get angry when the subject comes up."

"Mrs Cherry pays well," Gawain smiled. "And the going rate as well." She's very happy that Miss Clements and I tell folk stories to Raynard. She truely believes it helps the children to be good in all their school work."

"That's pride, isn't it. Pride in yourself."

"I don't think people who originally came from the Caribbean and are living here for a long time and have no intention of returning. I don't think just because these people don't talk about the Caribbean, they hate it. It might be they are homesick, frustrated. They feel wretched that they can't live in the Caribbean as they can live here. I mean, why talk about something you can't have!"

"That's a good point," Darwin conceded as he drained his cup. "I feel connected to the Caribbean not because my parents came from the Caribbean, but because I feel a very deep spiritual bond. We can also feel a connection to both countries."

"Oh, yes, that's true."

Suddenly they heard clicking sounds; then they noticed that the street outside was lit up brightly. They rushed to the window and saw hundreds or maybe thousands of little lights swarming along the street and over rooftops. It was as if stars had fallen from the sky.

"Oh, God, it's dem fireflies things, Gawain said in Caribbean language. "Where they come from, man?"

"Stay here for a minute" Darwin said enthusiastically. "I'm going to check it."

"Sure, yes, alright," Gawain answered as he glared out of the window.

Darwin quietly left the flat, went to the front door of the house, opened and closed it quietly, but instead of going outside into the street, he went quietly down to Rosita Clement's flat. He knocked on her door, there was no reply. He knocked again, a little louder, still no answer. He waited for about eight minutes, then he quietly skipped back upstairs, went to the front door again, opened it very quietly, stood on the steps, looking around in awe at the starry scene of fireflies. Nobody else was about. He then closed the door and went back to Annette's flat.

"What you see?" Gawain went on, eyes popping out of the window.

"Only a street filled with fireflies," Darwin's face hardened. "I can't understand it." He went to the window and looked out, but as he was looking out he was lost in thought.

"You know in the Caribbean they call them, 'Candle flies'!" Gawain marvelled. "But what the hell are they doing in England is beyond me!"

"What is your opinion about all this and all that's been going on in the area, Arthur? You must have some kind of opinion. Come on, tell me your thoughts on all this." Darwin's voice was laboured.

Gawain scratched his head, and when he spoke there was a tension in his voice.

"I think that it's the hot summers and mild winters we've been having that are causing these fireflies to appear," he said with a deep breath. "I know other people have said this and I agree with them. About the blood-sucking deaths, I think it's the work of a mad serial killer. Other people have said that too. I think that's the simple explanation."

"Maybe you are all right," Darwin sighed. "Maybe that's all it is."

And as they stared at the twinkling lights, suddenly all the lights swirled and came together to form one big ball of fire which shot off over the rooftops. The sky was dark and ominous. Dogs howled and howled until morning.

Four men met at least once a week in a dingy back room of a Community Centre in Ladbroke Grove. In these meetings they drank alcohol, smoked marijuana and talked about their sexual conquests. The seats in the room were dirty, tattered and broken. There was a stained mattress rolled up in a corner, a wooden box served as a table. The once cream-coloured walls were now discoloured by smoke. The only window with a broken and dirty pane, was never opened. Sometimes the men squatted on the torn dirty grey carpeted floor. They always assembled at night. A candle flickered in a saucer on the box.

One mid June night they were enjoying themselves high on marijuana and beer. As far as they were concerned, they were floating on air; the world was a magical place.

"She'll never leave me, I tell you!" said a small man. "I little but I well-endowed!"

The others laughed but laughter sounded like echoes to them.

"We know that, man!" said a tall man sitting on the floor. "Louise told me what you have God didn't give it to you."

They laughed again.

Each was smoking a marijuana-filled cigarette.

"I don't take any shit from women, you know!" said a huge man sprawled on the broken-down sofa. "When I give them my hard-earned money and I want to make love anytime, they have to give it to me anyway I want it, or else is blows." And he opened a can of beer and sipped.

A fat, pot-bellied one sat in an armchair without cushions, he continually sipped and smoked. "Well, women have to treat me nice, because I have money. I ain't rich, but I have some money saved, quite a lot of bread."

The small man unrolled the mattress and sat on it, and laughed, "Did I tell you all about how I did it in this room here on this mattress with Ethel."

The others' eyes rolled in disbelief.

"You don't mean, Ethel who works at the House Agents near the tube station. You can't mean Ethel!" said the tall man, puffing.

"But she thinks she's an angel," said the huge man. "She says she's only going to have sex when she gets married."

"You mean, she's a virgin!" the fat pot-bellied man stared bleary-eyed at the huge man.

With a sneer and large gulp of beer, the small man said, "Women talk nonsense most of the time. They lie all the time. When I opened her legs on this mattress, I found a big, free hole that could take in a motor-car."

The others laughed and laughed between smoking and drinking.

"And when they say no, they really mean, yes!" the tall man scowled and swallowed.

"I think women was created for man, to do everything for man," the huge man grunted.

"Yes. All this equality is shit!" the fat pot-bellied man was still laughing.

Suddenly all around the Community Centre screams were heard. It was as if the whole area was wailing. The wailing sky was bright but it changed to foreboding darkness.

A ball of fire about the size of a pigeon, began to hit against the window of the room.

They stared.

"Lightning, we're going to get a storm!" the small man's voice shook.

The fire-ball kept hitting the window.

"Listen to the wind!" the tall man sprang to his feet.

"Did you hear that scream?" the huge man sat up.

"It's dogs that's all!" The fat pot-bellied man went to the window.

The fire-ball now struck the window forcefully.

"That wind is going to break the window!" the fat pot-bellied man went to the window and placed his hand against it.

The fire-ball struck, and the window burst open and the fire-ball came in swirling and spinning around the room, over their heads, in between them, emitting a clicking sound.

"It's...it's...that...that...killer insect thing!" the tall man tried to grab the fire-ball.

The fire-ball swooped at his head and knocked him over, unconscious.

The small man and the fat pot-bellied man went for the door, but the fire-ball pounced on them in a flash and knocked them down.

"I'm not afraid of whatever you are!" the huge man posed like a boxer."Come, let me put your light out!" He moved around the room like a boxer in a ring, fists flying.

The fire-ball came at him, and for a moment he

thought he saw a woman's face, glowing through the flame, and he heard a voice exploding in his brain, "You pile of nastiness! Always talking shit! Wasting your lives! All your days are finished!" And it alighted on his throat and tore it out, the blood spilling all over the room.

Then it manifested into the skin-less female with long, wild hair, blood-red eyes, and a mouth with protruding teeth, and long claw-like finger nails. It went to the other three, bit their throats and stomachs out, drank their blood. Then it ripped off their penises and testicles, chewed them in a pap and spat it out all over the room. Then it chuckled, turned into a fire-ball again and flew out of the window.

Chapter Twelve

Darwin concentrated all his efforts on the area where Rosita Clements lived. He was sure he was closing in on the monster. Besides suspecting Rosita Clements; he also had his eye on another old woman who lived in a neighbouring street who also lived alone, had no friends and family, and never went out in the day-time. And on several occasions he had followed the firefly's light and it always came to that area.

It was mid August, the summer was hot like fire. The Carnival approached. Carnival fever swept through the area. Some people were shocked by the death of old Eddy, but that was put aside as everyone was gripped by Carnival planning and preparations:

Voices went up merrily:

• I want to be the best this year......

- It's more beautiful than last year....

- Nothing going to stop me from enjoying meself....

- We going to win a prize this year.....

- Carnival sweet like sugar....

- I wish everyday was Carnival....

- I like dat tune for de street......

- Sun hot jus' like back home.....

- My body start dancing already......

- This costume is going surprise everybody.....

- I wonder if de police go allow me to sell rum on de stall....

- It's green, velvet, braided with lace and lamé....

- I want de cape to look like wings.....

- De sewing-machine break down.....

- Borrow Auntie Marva's, it's a better one....

- Red, silver, gold, turquoise here....

- I drunk from now till Carnival.....

- Blue and silver again.....

- I selling peas and rice and chicken.....

- Come and try on this bodice......

- Mummy it's too tight around the waist.....

- What's happening, man. What you playing this year.......
- Dat's a secret, man, you know dat.....
- This is going to light up the street.....
- You must put a second coat of paint on it.....
- Yellow, blue and red satin....
- Man, it's so pretty when I move me hands.....
- I'll buy de beads and rhinestones from de same store......
- Play dat song again, I didn't get it de first time.....
- It'll sound so sweet on the steel band......
- Not only green wings but a green beak....
- I save up all me money just for it......
- I'll dance like this and this and this......
- Times hard and worrying, but Carnival is de sweetest thing....
- Where did you get money from to buy that......
- That's a better shape than last year...
- De children get so excited like is Christmas......
- Me head full up with Carnival.....
- All blood-sucking monster aside, I only thinking

of Carnival......

• Girl, me head too hot to worry about dat.......

Mrs Cherry was found dead at her home. Her body was drained of blood. The police couldn't understand how the killer got into her home because all the doors and windows were locked. She was watching television when she was attacked.

Raynard and Gawain were upset.

There was a meeting at the school.

Darwin felt that very soon he would unmask the killer.

Unlike Old Eddy's death; this time there was an uproar; a cold chill ran down the spines of people in the area. Some people thought it was a racist killing because of Mrs Cherry's views and ideas on multicultural education and racism. In cafes, shops, stores, street-stalls, pubs , offices, clubs, community centres, schools and on the streets, frightened people talked about the murder:

• Such a nice lady too......

• She use to teach me children......

• It's a bloody racist did that.....

- Yea, man, they don't want to see people get along......

- She'lll be sorely missed......

- We must dedicate this year's Carnival to her......

- She's like that.....

- It must be the best ever in honour of her......

- She liked black people so much......

- This Carnival should be Mrs Cherry's Carnival.....

- Dat woman always help everyone.....

- She's in heaven, the blessed soul.....

- It's me daughter favourite teacher, man.......

- Such an understanding woman......

- I don't think she ever got angry.....

- The police are dragging their feet with these murders.....

- What's needed is more police officers on the beat....

- Tragic, ain't it, mate.....

- Dem thief is gettin' more skilful everyday.....

- Property prices in this area have plummeted.....

- Only de other day I see she smiling happy face......

"Raynard liked her a lot," Annette couldn't hold back her tears which boiled inside her. "He's...he..he's so upset. I had to beg him to see his friends today....." she broke off.

Darwin embraced her.

"He told me she was the best teacher in the school", Gawain said with a lump in his throat.

As he embraced her, Darwin reflected, "Mrs Cherry lived not far from here, did she?"

"Yes, just around the corner, really. We're sort of neighbours. Ray told his friends that she was his neighbour." While Annette spoke she had a distant look in her eyes and her body trembled in Darwin's arms,

"I was thinking about Raynard taking part in the Carnival," Gawain ventured.

Annette pulled away from Darwin and almost snarled at Gawain, "There's a mad killer out there! It wouldn't be safe for Ray! They should postpone the Carnival this year!"

"I know that, but I'll be there, and the stewards and the police; we'd be there watching out for him," Gawain's voice was full of emotion. "Ray told me he'd love to wear a costume and dance in the streets. You can't take away the joy and happiness from people because some nut is going around thinking that he's Dracula!"

Annette fumed, her arms folded, her body still shaking,her head bowed.

"I agree with Gawain," Darwin said passionately.

"Darling, Ray will be perfectly safe. I'll be there as well watching out for him. I think Mrs Cherry would've wanted it. And he'll be so happy."

"I'll see what I can do about the costume," Gawain smiled. "It wouldn't be anything fussy. We don't have time to prepare anything elaborate. It'll have to be simple but beautiful."

"No, no, no, no, it's better to be safe than sorry!" Annette was adamant. "I mean he hasn't got over the shock of Mrs Cherry's death. How can you think of things like that at the present time!"

"Ray is a bright boy," Gawain was still smiling. "Nothing bad is going to happen to him. He always listens to good advice. Anyway, Annette, you think about it. You'll see it'll be alright. I'll see you later." He thought it might be a good idea to leave the two of them alone now. "Think carefully of what you'll be doing to the boy." And he left them.

When Raynard heard that his mother didn't want him to take part in the Carnival, his world fell apart. He was totally shattered. He cried and cried and fell asleep in a sea of tears. His sleep was full of disappointed dreams. Sleeping and waking, his life seemed in total chaos.

"Mummy, please, let me play!" he screamed in his dreams. The Carnival music rang in his head; he tossed and turned, woke, looked around his room wildly, fell asleep again and dreamt of colourful costumes dancing, singing and laughing. "Mummy, please, let me play!" his voice was lost in Carnival crowds. "Mummy, please, let me play!"

Annette and Darwin argued late into the night. It was their first argument.

"He's not your son!" Annette stormed at him. "You want him to be killed by the blood-sucking monster! I say he's not wearing any costume in the streets, and that's final!" and she came away from him and stood looking at the floor, shaking.

"Alright, Alright, if that's the way you want it!" Darwin said angrily as he went out to Gawain's flat.

"You know, I'll never understand women!" he sipped beer, a little perplexed.

"Some months ago, I told her it would be a great idea to let Ray take part in the Carnival, at least, take part in the Children's Carnival. She said it was alright and now she says no, she has changed her mind about Carnival," Darwin looked at his can of beer as if he was seeing it for the first time.

"Well, if dat's de way she feel, dat's it then."

Darwin frowned, "That's women's way, whatever we might think, they have a right to change their minds."

"I had a girlfriend like that once," Gawain mused, "She never said 'no' or 'yes' whenever I asked her something, she always said, 'maybe'."

"My father told me, my mother gave him the run-around," Darwin sighed after a gulp of beer. "He thought that she was never going to go out with him, let alone marry him."

"Annette's friend, Jocelyn, is the same," Gawain's voice was unsteady. "Most of the time, she's uncertain."

"I think the female sex is smarter than the male in everything," Darwin stood by the window, looking out as he spoke. It was a very hot night; Gawain had put on an electric fan. Darwin noticed a bird-like creature, he thought it was a pigeon, outside a window of the building. It was trying to get in.

"What the! What's that!!! It looks like a bird trying to get in...." and Darwin turned and rushed out of the flat.

Gawain rushed to the window.

Darwin realised that the window through which the bird-like creature was trying to get in was Annette's flat window; this window was opened with the blinds down. He raced to the flat; but there wasn't any sign of Annette. He went to her bedroom, she wasn't there. He went to Raynard's room and found the firefly, big as a bird, glowing and swirling around the room. Raynard was fast asleep. Darwin tried to catch it, but it was too swift for him. He chased it around and out of the room; he was sweating profusely. Finally, with the greatest effort he managed to slam the window shut with the firefly outside.

Raynard slept through the whole incident; he wasn't harmed in any way.

Darwin looked out of the window and wondered where Annette could be. He collected himself and began to toss the various things over in his mind, first on his agenda was Rosita Clements. He was thinking of going to check her out in the basement when Annette came through the flat door with a worried look on her face.

"Where were you? I've been looking.....I..."Darwin's voice seemed to echo.

Annette looked about her strangely and replied, "I was upset after our row. I went downstairs to Miss Clements. I knocked and knocked on her door, but although a light was on, I didn't get any answer."

"There was a firefly in the flat a while ago," Darwin controlled his anxiety. "It was strange. It flew about the rooms. I tried to catch it, but it was too fast for me. It got out again through the window."

"Well, ha, what are you talking about!" Annette almost laughed. "I think you had too much beer at Gawain's."

"No, dear, I know what I saw," Darwin softened. "It was a bit terrifying, flying about Ray's room."

"I must say it's hot like Caribbean weather," now she laughed sarcastically. "It's true what some say, the hot summer is bringing strange insects from Africa and the Caribbean."

It's no joke, I'm serious ," Darwin surveyed her closely. "You know, I wouldn't joke about such things."

"Not to worry, I tell you, its the heat," And Annette looked away.

And I think its that blasted succubus in the basement, thought Darwin.

The following morning a scream was heard from Gawain's flat. It was Rosita screaming.

Annette and Darwin rushed to the flat to find Rosita standing over Gawain's body which showed a wound in the throat and around his groin was covered in blood.

Darwin was very careful as he examined the body.

His mind swam in conflicting thoughts. He knew that whatever or whoever the killer was; its lair or hiding place was somewhere between where Mrs Cherry and Gawain were murdered.

"He's dead. I think all the blood has been drained from his body," Darwin stood up, hands on hips, looking around the room.

"Oh, Gawd! Oh, Gawd, Oh, de poor man!" Rosita sobbed like a child. "I come to give 'im some clean pillow cases and sheet. And me find 'im on the floor bleeding bad, bad. Oh, poor Gawain, poor soul".

Darwin watched her carefully, then he phoned the police.

Gawain's body was taken away. His relatives were notified. The police made a thorough search of the house inside and outside.

When Jocelyn heard she fainted and when she came to, she was beside herself with shock and worry. She was never the same again. "Oh Jesus! We should've been married! He loved me. I know it. At first he was like a little boy. But he was a kind man. He always treated me well."

Her life from then was spent in a sobbing, mournful state. At Gawain's funeral she threw herself on his coffin, and had to be restrained from throwing herself in the grave.

Annette thought that she was over-doing it.

Many people in the area were shaken by the tragic death of Gawain. Although the incident gave the Carnival fever a jolt, it couldn't stop it. Most people thought that Gawain would've wanted it to carry on in the greatest splendour and happiness regardless of what tragedy occurred. People also thought that the coming Carnival should be a tribute to Mrs Cherry and Gawain.

"I think as a mark of respect," Darwin was going to suggest it no matter what. "Since Arthur was to play a leading part in the Carnival, Raynard should do it. Otherwise, the costume will go to waste. Arthur would've wanted it that way."

It was a beautiful sunny August Saturday afternoon. Besides Darwin and Annette, Jocelyn and Rosita were also present. Raynard was in his room with a friend.

Annette was sitting, she got up, frowned and pushed the seat away angrily. "I've told you no already.

How many times do I have to say, no, no, no, no, no!"

Jocelyn sighed as if a great burden was taken off her shoulders. "That's....that's...yes... I see...it's a good idea, yes....I've been thinking.....yes."

Rosita went to calm Annette, and agreed, "Yes, me was thinking de same thing. Gawain spirit go watch over 'im!"

Jocelyn cleared her throat, "It's the right thing to do. Why waste such a beautiful costume like that. Let him take part, Ann, Please!"

Darwin smiled broadly, "I've told you he'll be alright," he said and went and cuddled Annette.

Annette pulled away from him, "Alright, he can take part, let him wear the costume and dance himself silly. The three of you are satisfied now! But if anything happens to him, it'll be on your heads! And another thing, I'm not going to watch him when he's dancing in the streets. You can go on your own!"

"But I've told you before," Darwin laughed drily. I'll look after Ray."

Jocelyn and Rosita looked at each other.

Darwin could sense a rage that boiled in Annette. Something was ready to explode, but he wasn't going to let it. He moved towards her, opened his arms and she fell into them.

Raynard was the happiest boy in the world; he boasted to his friends.

Chapter Thirteen

The Notting Hill Carnival came with a bang! It was one of the best ever. There were bigger bands and more individuals in colourful, inventive costumes. Long ribbons of calypso, reggae and soul music blasted the air. The streets were flamed with colour! Everyone was breathing in the music. The streets and pavements were jam packed with people. There was smiling, laughing, dancing and singing everywhere. It was an intensely hot, bright day.

Velvet, satin, silk, shone into silver, gold and crimson. Stars glittered the day time. Dancers reeled, jumped and rolled in the air and on ground. Smiles lit up the whole area. Laughter came into house where sadness had reigned. Drums beat and seemed to burst with the excitement of the rhythms of the streets. Songs rose from lips in a chorus together. As the music surged, everyone was transformed into a masquerade whether they wore a costume or not. The sweet sounds of the Carnival hypnotised all in complete abandonment.

Green and blue wings of bats, butterflies, birds and grasshoppers. Red beaks of hawks and eagles. The rhythm of turquoise on yellow swans-down. Beads of braiding trimmed with lace and green velveteen came up streets and melted into a sea of sky-blue heads with banana-yellow bodies. Steel bands boomed the magic of the day. Lilac and purple skipped along gracefully.

The pavements vendors with their fried chicken, peas and rice, other boiled and steamed food and refreshing drinks, grinned as the delicious smells leapt into the nostrils of the crowds.

The sounds of colour and colours of sounds sparkled in the faces of children, wiping away all tears and fear. Fairytale characters came alive on the streets. Mickey Mouse danced with Tom and Jerry. Children dressed in coats of tigers and leopards. Skins of snakes, feathers of peacocks and scarlet ibises.

There were costumes of: a vampire blood-sucking

bats, clad in purple velvet with huge wings on roller stakes; a green and turquoise mosquito, and a leech of black satin and silk with a great mouth and long tongue. As the music blasted and boomed, these masquerades moved in the streets and amongst the crowds and pretended to suck peoples' blood. To some it was all a joke, fun; but to others it was in bad taste and insensitive.

Darwin thought that the best masquerade of all was the woman who changed into the blood-sucking Soucouyant creature; that person was walking around the streets, admiring the costumes, and even dancing, but dancing to a different kind of rhythm, a rhythm of blood.

The Bat-Masquerade came along. Spectators gave it room, some cheered and clapped! Tourists took photographs, then it stuck out its tongue and wiggled it. Some spectators and other masqueraders laughed.

The excitement of the crowds soared!

Raynard felt as if he was walking on air; as he moved along the street he seemed to float. His hummingbird costume which was taking in here and there from Gawain's size to fit him, fitted him smartly. His face was shining with smiles.

As Darwin watched Raynard he felt as if Raynard's steps were somehow guided by the inspirations of Gawain. Although when he thought of Gawain he felt sad, the sadness was never going to overcome him because of the complete happiness which swept over Raynard. As he thought about how Gawain might have moved in the turquoise, satin and blue velvet hummingbird costume; Raynard began to dance, his whole body moved in time with the rhythm of the music. The tragedy of Gawain's death wasn't going to take over as he watched Raynard making the costume his, and dance-steps that Gawain would've been proud of. As far as Darwin was concerned Raynard was a shining hummingbird, a radiant creature of flight, emitting silver bits around the wings and breast. It was extraordinary how he fitted into Gawain's costume so perfectly. Rosita and Jocelyn had done a great job on the costume.

As Darwin watched the costumes, he remembered the Caribbean folktales Gawain told him. Gawain had said that it was all superstition, but some people especially the old, believed that some of the tales were based on fact.

Every dragon's and devil's face were grinning at him with red tongues dangling.

Raynard danced his heart out.

Darwin kept his eyes on him.

There were cheers, whistles and clapping.

There more police than usual patrolling the streets.

Darwin felt a tap on his shoulder, he turned and recognised Jocelyn.

"Ray is a great dancer!" she smiled and shouted above the roar of the crowd. "I didn't know he could move like that!"

"Me too, he must be a quick learner!" Darwin smiled and raised his voice as well.

They pushed along, following the dancing, smiling and happy hummingbird that was Raynard.

An hour or so later, they stopped so that Raynard could have some refreshment. They were also thirsty. Then they were off again, through the crowded streets of glittering faces; sound systems blasting, bodies gyrating and steel bands enticing.

The sky was blue and bright. The sun was also enjoying itself.

Raynard met friends and teachers from his school who hailed and complimented him.

"Hi Ray, it's wicked!" sang a boy with his parents.

"Raynard, you're looking simply wonderful!" shouted a teacher with her male companion who was smiling broadly.

"Mummy look it's Raynard from my school in the hummingbird costume!" a girl shrieked, pointing and holding tightly onto her mother's hand. The mother stared wide-eyed, smiling and nodding.

"Have a nice day Raynard!" a bearded young man called out.

Darwin, Jocelyn and Raynard stopped again and had fried chicken, peas and rice and more cold drinks.

The day turned to late afternoon.

Darwin suddenly began to think of Rosita Clements. Many times he had probed her mind with silly, simple things and she had always found ways to change the subject. Maybe what Gawain told about him the

Soucouyant vampire, touched her most sensitive nerve. Maybe she thought Gawain had discovered her secret and that was why she killed him. Yes, thought Darwin, Rosita Clements fitted the description of the Soucouyant perfectly. It if wasn't her, then it must be one of her neighbours. He steeled himself, turned to Jocelyn and said loudly, "Please, look after Ray for me! I won't be long!" He had to repeat himself before Jocelyn understood clearly, and she nodded her agreement.

Steel bands rang out the sweetest tunes! Laughter cheers! Darwin began to push and fight his way through the thick crowds. The thoughts swam through his mind: Annette was alone in her flat, alone with Rosita Clements! He had to get to her quickly! He had to save his beloved Annette from the evil blood-sucking Soucouyant! The monster was going to devour his beloved! He pushed in an alleyway, quiet and away from the thunder of the Carnival, switched on his mobile and rang Annette but no one answered the phone! His heart began to drum like the steel bands! He had to hurry! He pushed himself out of the alleyway, and began to battle his way through the vast crowd; he pushed this way and that way! The crowd followed the beautiful costumes and the intoxicating music of the bands. He was sucked into a group of dancing butterflies with blue and red wings, spotted with yellow: they blocked his passage; they giggled and playfully patted his head and shoulders. He swore silently at all flying creatures. There were cheers and more cheers all around for the dancers in their stunning, eye-popping costumes. Then a huge wall of people were moving in the opposite direction to him. It seemed impossible to get through. He pushed and pushed against it. He struggled, swayed and swayed and almost fell over and under their feet. But he was strong and persistent.

It was as if a great tidal wave was sweeping through the area. Everyone was lost in the spirit of Carnival. Rosita or someone near her was wearing a human costume and fooling everybody! He had to get Annette before it was too late! He was swimming in the sea of revellers. He shouted and pulled at arms, clothes and other body parts. This was Carnival, the theatre of the streets, maybe even the theatre of life.

"Play mas!" a man's voice bawled.

"That's sexy, darling!" shouted another.

"De man really really handsome, you know!" a woman swooned.

A child was crying.

"Come and take a drink, man!" A man laughed. The steel bands banged deep.

A Siren sang out!

Mobiles rang. Few were heard.

The streets were lit up like a Christmas tree.

Red Riding Hood held hands with the Wolf; Donald Ducked waved to Peter Pan; Pinocchio danced with Harry Potter; Purple spiders embraced multicoloured flies stretched from street to street. A banner of a giant mouth with blood-red lips heralded a band of daffodil costumes. Grey and silver aliens held ray-guns reflecting sunlight. Shapes and weavings of gold, bronze and silver highlighted moon, planets, stars and space-ships.

Calypso sang with reggae and salsa. Bob Marley strummed away!

Cheers and laugher! A Siren sang out!

Finally, Darwin swan his way out of the current filled sea of revellers. His brain was racked with infinite possibilities of who could be the blood sucking Soucouyant! He couldn't take most of them, he dispelled them quickly. The music followed him as he raced to his beloved's home!

He made his way to the street, dashed to the house; opened the door, raced to Annette's flat, but she wasn't there. His heart beat like a frienzied drum. Carnival music sang in his ears! Maybe Annette had decided to go to the Carnival after all. He made his way down to Rosita's darkened basement flat. The floorboards creaked, shadows sprang up on the walls, a light came in from outside. The shadows seemed to do a skeleton dance. He thought he heard a scream, and then like someone choking. The place smelt of rotting rubbish. Then he thought he heard a ghost-like cry, then a growl, then a cry of pain. A creaking door or window seemed to be opening, then a sucking, slurping sound. The Carnival music, shouts, cheers and laughter filled the surroundings. He kept his mind focused.

Rosita's door opened slowly and creaked. The sucking slurping sound stopped. He stumbled forward towards her doorway, his heart racing but he wasn't afraid. The place was dark and creepy. He wasn't sure if she was there or not, so he called out, "Miss Clements, are you there? Are you alright?" This was done more for courtesy because he felt he was intruding.

The thick black curtains in the window were closed. He discovered a gruesome sight that seemed to bear out his worse fears. On the floor next to a large, old opened suitcase was a white basin with what looked like a human skin in blood –red liquid. That must be the skin of the Soucouyant thought Darwin as his eyes popped at the hideous sight as he tried to come to terms with what Gawain had told him. It was like a terrible nightmare. The door closed behind him. He turned his head, there stood the crazed figure of Rosita Clements, her eyes wild, red and staring.

She screamed as she waved a machete. He hardly recognised her in this wild state, and first he thought that this was Rosita in her Soucouyant mask. But on careful examination he realised that this was the real Rosita Clements and that she was terrified.

"What! You! "Rosita was surprised to see Darwin.

I'm sorry, I came into your flat like this! But the door was opened, and I came to check for Ann..."

Darwin stopped.

"Come to check here, she don't live here!" Rosita was suspicious.

"Well, for a start, how do you explain this?" And Darwin pointed to the white basin and its grisly secrets. "The owner of this skin is the beast that has been terrorising the area," he came straight to the point. "I'm concerned for the safety of Annette and her son. I don't want any harm to come to them. I'll do everything in my power to protect them. To think that this evil is right under their noses, makes me very angry."

Rosita sighed heavily, put down the machete and laughed deeply.

"That ain't no Soucouyant-skin! You talking stupidness! That skin was there long, long time. I think it might be de skin of a animal dead long ago. I was cleaning and one of de floorboards was loose and when I moved it, I find the skin there. Maybe it was a pet animal de people who was living here before me had. And it dead and they bury it under the floor to be near them always. Or maybe it's de skin of a baby a mother didn't want. I don't know what skin it is. When I find it it was dry, dry. There wasn't no blood nowhere. I mean, no blood-stain or nothing. I confuse. I frightened like hell."

I can't understand!" Darwin was puzzled. "Why didn't you report it to the police?"

"I don't want nothing to do with no police in dis country, man. After all dat's been happening, some people will say I is de blood sucker. De skin is in my place, dat's all de proof they go want," Rosita's face lost all its colour.

"They go have to proof it!" Darwin broke into Caribbean language. "Come on, man, Use you senses. You is a grown woman!" His voice was sharper than a knife.

Voices outside swelled!

Through loud-speakers, guitars throbbed calysoes sweet!

Rosita's heart-strings were playing a different tune. A reggae chorus filled the air.

"You....you...you..think...oh Gawd," Rosita felt a tightness in her stomach, she began to pace.

Darwin probed the skin with his pen.

"Yes, I understand!" she spurted out. "You is a educated man. You think de person who's going around killing people and sucking their blood is Soucouyant and dat is they skin! Or you think the killer kill dis person and put it here to make it look like is me who do de killing. Yes, all de blood suck out. I must use me head and think careful, man. But...but...I don't understand what going on. Soucouyant is fairytale. Dat can't be happening in London." She swayed and swayed but steadied herself. "Den, den, I...we must put salt on de skin and put raw rice grain all over the place, as it say in de stories in de Caribbean...."

"I know, yes, Gawain told me all about it," Darwin agreed. "I don't think it's animal skin nor a baby's. We have to be careful." But if Rosita wasn't the blood sucking killer? Maybe someone is trying to frame her, a feuding neighbour, perhaps? Darwin had conflicting thoughts. It couldn't be Rosita's because she wouldn't have wanted salt to be put on it, and raw rice grains to be spread around. Why is the skin hidden in Rosita's flat? Darwin's perceptive mind seemed to penetrate the flat, searching for clues, answers!

Outside a riot of melody! Singing arose higher and higher!

"Who it is must come to get they skin,"Rosita said mournfully. "But me don't understand. I thought de Soucouyant only came out in de night."

"Things change, man," Darwin into his Caribbean voice.

"Whoever it is , has to change because they're operating in new surroundings. They got to adapt, man. Let's wait and see, eh!" Darwin's mind was wide open as ever. "We go soon find out how true them Caribbean story is. It could be a crazy killer who is using de soucouyant and vampire behaviour to confuse and frighten de police. Maybe it's just a serial killer on de loose as some people say. But there is some very strange things going on in dis world"

Jubilant voices sang heartily!

Steel bands scattered piercing notes!

Cheers, laughter and clapping!

Rosita slumped in an armchair, her face worn, her eyes faraway. Then she sprang to her feet, and she and Darwin with rubber gloves on, began putting salt on the old, gnarled human skin. Then they poured raw rice grains all over the floor around it. Darwin had always been ready with salt and raw rice grains after what Gawain told him about the Soucouyant myth.

The haunting tone of an electric piano curled its salsa all around the house.

Rosita was gloomy and blinded with tears.

Darwin's eyes were full of wonder.

Sweet sonorous chants harmonised outside.

Darwin and Rosita heard a movement in the hallway. Their hearts were racing. They heard a familiar voice. It was Annette's, as she called out, "Miss Clements! Has Darwin come back? Where are you? What are you doing?"

Darwin was relieved to know that she was safe. He and Rosita rushed out, but was confronted by a terrible sight. The most horrible revelation greeted him: the blood-sucking killer, the Soucouyant, was his beloved, Annette. She had just killed again and was covered in blood. She had thought that the Carnival would hide her. She had had a blood feast.

Rosita almost collapsed.

In spite of what was happening around him, Darwin managed to keep his cool.

"Oh, Gawd, oh!" Rosita bawled. "Raynard father didn't leave dem. I bet she kill 'im and hide de body down here in me room when I wasn't here. Lawd, Jesus! All de time it down here. De child growing up thinking he father left dem. When all de time he body in me room rottening away. Almighty Gawd, help us!"

So the Soucouyant was very real. Darwin was totally broken up, but he wasn't afraid. His beloved Annette was the killer. She had the power to turn into fireflies. It was fascinating, but monstrous. It was beyond all human endurance. His throat was full of choking as he said,

"Ann...ette....I...I..can't...believe it. You...you...fooled us all...You....you...are the thing responsible for all the deaths in this place. For God's sake, think of your son. He has been living with a monster looking after him. You've.... you've...tricked us all. Ray was in danger all the time. What has...what has happened to you...you...seemed to be so good...so.." He stared in horror.

Annette or what I looked like Annette, wore a bright flowered dress, a wig of dreadlocks and a smiling face mask. She now ripped off the dress, wig and mask, and stood before them, leering with a leech-like tongue, blood red eyes, white hair, skinless with a withered old face, then the face changed to that of Annette's pretty young face, sneering, "Yes, it's me! I hate all men! They kill my mother! They always fool and hurt me! So I asked the devil for long life, youth and beauty, and he gave it to me. I've lived a very long life, from the days when the evil men took us as slaves from Africa to the Caribbean. I cursed them all, and vowed to get revenge! And I was going alright until an interfering, clever son of a pig like you came along!"

174

Darwin tried to work it all out: maybe she can't help herself, maybe a curse was put on her? Maybe she's mad and needs psychological help? All kinds of thoughts raced through his brain. In this day and age how could all this be true? Gawain was killed because he knew too much about the Soucouyant myth. But what about Rosita Clements? Why wasn't she murdured?

Rosita herself was shaking all over.

The hideous creature that was masquerading as Annette rushed past them and went to Rosita's flat. Rosita staggered and almost fell over but was helped by Darwin.

"Are you alright, Miss Clements?" his voice was strained.

"Yes, me in shock, but I fine. Man, let we go quick to she! I sure she woulda kill me when she feel she didn't have uses for me. All this time me life was in danger! I love she like me own daughter. How she could do dis in me place!"

"And all de time I think it was you," Darwin was in Caribbean language again.

They went quickly back to Rosita's flat. They came

upon the hideous sight bending over the old gnarled skin, groaning, "I found out I could come out in the day time. But I didn't because I would easily be seen. The dark of night hides everything. Raw rice grains don't work anymore. But...but....salt on my skin...oh, no..no.. I can't touch it...it burns me...Skin, skin, come to me! Skin don't you know me! Oh, Lucifer, where are you!" Then it let out an agonising howl, cringed, fell on the floor, shrivelled and died before their amazed eyes.

The Carnival music, laughter and colour blazed on and on outside. The loudest cheers and applause echoed all around.

"I give she de keys and free run of me basement!" Rosita raged on and wet herself. "And dis is what she do to me! You can't trust nobody these days!"

With all his might, Darwin held back the feeling to vomit. But he couldn't hold back the tears. "All this is so irrational, man," he muttered.

BY THE SAME AUTHOR

NOVELS

SIGNPOSTS OF THE JUMBIE
THE BLACK MAGIC MAN OF BRIXTON
JUMBIE STOLE THE INNOCENCE

STORIES

TALES FROM THE WEST INDIES
UNCLE CHARLIE'S CRICK CRACK TALES

POETRY

THE EXPATRIATE
CRAB TRACK
DAYS AND NIGHTS IN THE MAGIC FOREST
CHILDREN OF THE MORNING
SEA POEM

FOR CHILDREN

THE SELFISH CROCODILE
THE SELFISH CROCODILE NURSERY RHYME BOOK
ED. A CARIBBEAN COUNTING BOOK
ED. KISKADEE QUEEN
ED. UNDER THE STORYTELLER'S SPELL
WILKIE AND THE BAKOO
ANANCY MAN (OPERETTA)
GREEDY SNAKE
TEACHER ALLIGATOR
ONCE UPON AN ANIMAL